"It was [...]
Trevor [...]
room th[...]
and bu[...]
arranged along [...]
pitchforks and ha[...]
is riding by the light of the full moon."

"Wow! I've never done that before! It sounds amazing!"

"The moon will be full soon. Maybe we could go then?"

Kate felt a shiver of excitement run through her. What an adventure that would be, she thought.

Trevor pushed the wheelbarrow up to the first stall. He and Kate began shoveling muck into it, and they worked comfortably, side by side. Kate knew she must look terrible by now with bits and pieces of hay in her tangled hair and sweat running down her face, but it felt nice to be working with Trevor. He was easy to be around.

"I certainly never knew mucking out stalls could be so much fun," Trevor said and laughed. "I think I have you to thank for this, Miss Wiley."

Kate giggled and tossed more muck in the wheelbarrow. "And I, Mr. Williams, must thank you for a delightful time."

"We'll have to do this again sometime," Trevor said with fake solemnity.

"Yeah, in about an hour at the other end of the barn," Kate deadpanned.

"Oh woe, you obviously don't have the soul of a true romantic," said Trevor with mock despair.

"Smelly hay and horse muffins do not inspire romance," said Kate, carrying out the charade. "Let's talk white sand beaches and picnics at sunset."

"And moonlit rides," said Trevor.

The BLUE RIBBON series, published by Bantam Books:

1. RIDING HIGH
2. A HORSE OF HER OWN
3. KATE'S CHALLENGE

Coming soon:

4. GOLDEN GIRL

BLUE RIBBON 3
KATE'S
CHALLENGE
Chris St. John

BANTAM BOOKS
TORONTO · NEW YORK · LONDON · SYDNEY · AUCKLAND

BLUE RIBBON 3: KATE'S CHALLENGE

A BANTAM BOOK 0 553 400398

First published as a Fawcett Girls Only Book in USA by
Ballantine Books, a division of Random House, Inc., New York;
and simultaneously in Canada by Random House of Canada
Limited Toronto

First publication in Great Britain

PRINTING HISTORY
Bantam edition published 1990

Bantam Books are published by Transword Publishers Ltd.,
61-63 Uxbridge Road, Ealing, London W5 5SA, in Australia
by Transworld Publishers (Australia) Pty. Ltd., 15-23 Helles
Avenue, Moorebank, NSW 2170, and in New Zealand
by Transworld Publishers (N.Z.) Ltd., Cnr. Moselle and
Waipareira Avenues, Henderson, Auckland.

Made and printed in Great Britain by
BPCC Hazell Books
Aylesbury, Bucks, England
Member of BPCC Ltd.

Chapter 1

"WOULD you just take a look at this," Jessie said, stepping back to admire the bridle she was saddle-soaping. Its soft leather glowed in the light of the tack room, and Jessie's eyes sparkled the same rich brown color.

Dara looked up from the saddle she was hard at work cleaning, and pushed her tangle of blond curls out of her face.

"Wow! That old bridle hasn't looked that good since last year's horse trials," she said and grinned. "Thanks, Jess."

"What do you think, Kate?" asked Jessie. "Am I going to win the saddle-soaper of the year award, or what?"

Kate scrubbed away at her saddle that was laid upside down in the special cleaning rack. Her short nails were gummed up with grime and saddle soap. She worked intently, attacking the ridges of horse sweat and hair that seemed glued to its underside.

"Yoo-hoo, Ms. Wiley," sang out Jessie teasingly. "You've been selected to judge the world famous saddle-soaping contest, held this year at the prestigious Windcroft Stables of Smithfield, Connecticut. Now, if you'd just turn your attention this way please to exhibit A, a particularly beautiful example of a snaffle bridle."

Kate looked up, her blue eyes filling her tired, drawn face. Wisps of blond hair, pulled loose from her long ponytail made many hours before, drifted around her face like a spiderweb floating on the breeze. She smiled.

"Sorry, I was miles away."

"Let me guess," said Dara. "About two hundred fifty miles away in northern, no ... no ... southern ... yes ... southern ... Idaho? no ..." Dara put her index fingers on each temple, closed her eyes and began wandering dramatically around the tack room. "Yes, yes, I can see it all now. You're in southern *Vermont* ... at Tommy Langwald's combined training summer camp. You've been selected to attend, one of only fifteen riders from across the United States, because of your superior equestrian talents."

Jessie giggled.

Kate tossed her cleaning sponge at Dara, hitting her squarely in the back. "Okay, okay, so I'm a little anxious."

"A little anxious!" Jessie laughed. "I haven't been able to have a decent conversation with you since you were accepted to that place."

"Since all three of us were accepted," corrected Kate, flipping her saddle over and absentmindedly rubbing on more soap. She knew every flap and plane of that old saddle. There was the deep gouge it got the time she and Night Owl plowed through the rails at the Hillsborough Trials, and the scrape along the skirt where it had fallen off Night Owl that time he took off before she'd done up the girth.

"Well, I'm really looking forward to it," said Dara. "I think we're ready for this sort of super-intense workout."

Kate looked at her friend. How could she be so cool? Her own stomach had been flip-flopping all day, ever since she and her mother had had that talk after breakfast.

"Katie May," her mother had said as she picked up the dirty dishes from the table, "tomorrow you leave for Langwald's and a whole new experience."

"I'll just be working on the same old stuff you've been drilling into me for years, Mom. What can be so different about that?"

"Well, for starters, you're not a novice eventer anymore. This is your first year at the training level and I think you've seen from the two trials you've been in so far this summer that it's another kettle of fish."

"But Mom, Night Owl and I have done just fine. You've done a great job training me."

Anne Wiley smiled warmly at her daughter and began filling the sink with hot, soapy water. "Thank you, my sweet. But those two trials were local events. At Langwald's you'll be riding with kids from all over the country who'll be on horses that have been finely tuned in combined training for years. Horses like Northern Spy that are worth thousands of dollars. And for good reason. They perform."

Kate had felt instantly defensive. Why did every conversation come around to how wonderful and amazing Northern Spy was? Why was everyone from Pietro Yon to Dara and Jessie always trying to pawn Northern Spy off on her? Okay, so he was a good horse. A great horse. Kate got shivers remembering the one time she'd ridden him, how he'd responded so effortlessly to her most subtle command. It was like floating on a cloud. And he had spirit, too. He was noble and proud. But Night Owl was *her* horse. They were a team and they were going to the top. All the way. They had rows and rows of ribbons on the wall of the stable's office to prove it.

"Will you be able to handle all the work around here without me?" Kate had asked her mother, switching the subject. She placed the rinsed dishes carefully into the dishwasher.

"Oh, I think so," Anne had said. "Jessie's offered me all her free time and the doctor said my leg should be in shape to start some easy riding in another week or so."

Kate and her mother had worked silently for a few minutes, then Anne reached over and smoothed Kate's hair back from her forehead. "I'll miss you though, Katie May. It's tough having my baby leave home for the first time."

Kate had swallowed hard and willed herself not to cry. Of all the things about Langwald's riding camp that gave her butterflies, leaving her parents and home distressed her the most. Her parents had started this boarding-and-training stable when she was barely out of diapers. She'd spent her whole life here. She loved the old house with its creaks and groans and radiators that popped and fizzled. And, with her intense training schedule, she'd never even slept over at a friend's before. When she'd been gone for a two- or three-day event, one of her parents had always been with her. At Langwald's, she'd be on her own.

"I'll miss you, too, Mom," she had said, swallowing again. "But, don't you worry. I don't care how amazing those other kids are going to be, I'm going to show them that Anne Wiley of Windcroft Stables is the best combined-training instructor in the whole United States. I'll show 'em. I'll bring home every ribbon they've got to offer. Just you wait."

Anne had laughed. "Just work hard and have a good time. It's going to be one tough camp." She ran a sponge over the counters. "Now, if you don't get out to that barn and get to work, you'll still be there at midnight tonight."

Kate glanced at the clock on the wall of the tack room and saw that it was eight-thirty. She, Dara and Jessie had been at it almost nonstop since nine o'clock that morning—bathing the horses; cleaning out the horse van; helping Matthew, the farrier, trim the horses' hooves and shoe them; packing, and now saddle-soaping their saddles and bridles and halters. Kate was ready to drop.

The sound of a car coming up the driveway made them all pause. It crunched to a halt in the gravel outside the stables and a second later a tall, lithe, sandy-haired boy popped into the tack room. The summer sun had made his freckles stand out across his nose. Kate's spirits sagged. It wasn't Pete as she'd hoped, but Doug, Dara's boyfriend.

"Well, it's the three musketeers burning the midnight oil," he said, and smiled broadly.

Dara's eyes lit up. She crossed the room and gave him a quick hug. "Hi! I'm almost finished. Maybe another half hour or so."

"Another half hour! I was hoping to make the nine o'clock movie at the mall."

Dara fidgeted with the sponge in her hand. "Doug, we're leaving early tomorrow. I need to finish up this work." She looked at him, her blue eyes wide with pleading. "Couldn't we just go somewhere and get a burger or something. You know ... talk. I'm not going to see you for a month."

"Hey! You promised to come back for the dance at the club," protested Doug.

"I did not promise," countered Dara. "Who knows what's going to be happening at Langwald's."

Doug shifted from one foot to the other, clearly irritated. "Well, let's head out of here now. Maybe we can get through our burgers before you fall asleep like last Saturday."

"I'd been riding all day," Dara objected. "I was exhausted."

"Yeah," said Doug. "I lose out to a horse. That makes me feel real great. *Real* great."

Dara glanced nervously at Jessie and Kate. They concentrated on their work.

"Okay," said Dara quietly. "I'll come back early tomorrow and finish up here. Do you guys mind?"

"No problem," said Jessie and Kate almost in unison.

"What time do we leave in the morning?" asked Dara, packing away her saddle-soaping kit.

"We should be out of here by nine-thirty," said Kate.

"Okay. I'll be here at eight-thirty," replied Dara. She washed her hands at the sink in the corner and shook them dry. "You'll be here to see us off, won't you, Jess?"

"You bet," Jessie replied. "Balloons, white hankies, brass bands, tears. The works."

Dara laughed. "See you tomorrow then."

"Give our regards to Smithfield," sang out Kate.

"Remember us to Dawson Mall," chimed in Jessie.

"We might as well finish off Dara's stuff for her while we're on a roll," said Kate, moving over to her friend's saddle. Jessie joined her. They worked without speaking for a while, their world filled with the sounds of horses settling down for the night—snorts, stompings, the swish of hay being pulled from racks for a little midnight snack—and tree frogs and crickets outside blasting forth their own Hallelujah Chorus. To Kate these were the reassuring noises of home. She even recognized Night Owl's distinctive soft rumblings that told her he was feeling pretty good about life just then. Kate smiled. Good old Night Owl. Funny how you could love an animal so much.

"Do you think Dara and Doug are going to make it?" Jessie asked a few minutes later.

"Funny," said Kate, "I was just starting to think about them, too."

"And? . . ."

"They seem to really care for each other," said Kate.

"It's just hard to find time for anything but horses in this business," Jessie remarked.

"That's for sure," said Kate. "Seems like every time Pete and I plan something, the horses work out some plot to screw it up." Kate dampened a rag and rubbed Dara's stirrups. "Last week it was Miss Holly and her colic."

"But you told me Pete offered to come out and help you walk her," Jessie said.

"I know," Kate replied. "But I couldn't let him do that. You know how boring it is to walk a horse around and around for hours."

"I bet Pete would have made it fun," said Jessie. "He might not know anything about horses but he seems to like them."

Kate worked on silently for a moment, thinking how wonderful Pete had been at the last horse trials. His warm, eager face drifted before her mind. She smiled. "Yeah, you're right. He probably would have."

"That's where Pete and Doug are so different," Jessie continued. "Doug's always trying to take Dara away from horses, it seems, but Pete just about explodes with pride every time he watches you ride."

The smile on Kate's face widened. She glanced out the window.

"Is Pete coming out tonight?" asked Jessie.

"He said he'd try," Kate said. "But he had a big feed delivery somewhere in New York State which was going to get him back pretty late."

The girls labored on to finish Dara's saddle.

"You should be going to Langwald's with us tomorrow," said Kate with a final swipe of the sponge over the saddle. "I still can't believe you finked out on us."

"You know I'd be there if I could take Time Out, but Tip-Toe can't be weaned for another month, maybe two."

"You could take Jonathan. Mother would love you to work her horse. Or Northern Spy."

"You're doing it again, Kate," warned Jessie teasingly.

"You mean I can't even encourage you anymore?" Kate asked.

"Encourage, yes. Control my life, no."

"Humph," snorted Kate. "Then, let me just say I'd like to encourage you to reconsider and come to Langwald's with us. We've been planning on this all year."

"I know. I know," said Jessie. "But how did I know that Time Out wouldn't be able to come. Plus, now that the Jespers have agreed to sell her to me, I've got to stay here and make some money to pay for her. I mean, big bucks."

Silence settled in as they focused on their work once more.

"But what am I going to do without you?" blurted out Kate finally.

Jessie looked up in surprise. "What do you mean?"

"We've always been a team, Jess. I help you, you help me. How am I going to handle this boot camp of combined training, as people so sweetly call Langwald's, without you?"

Jessie put her hands on her hips and leaned her slender frame back into the cleaning rack. Her face was pale with exhaustion, making her dark hair seem even darker. "Why, Kate Wiley, you're going to go up there and knock 'em dead. You're great. You're one of the best. You're Kate Wiley of Windcroft Stables." She hesitated, then reached out and took Kate's arm. "You're Jessie Robeson's best friend, and I believe in you and know you're going to be terrific."

"Thanks, Jess," said Kate quietly. "I needed to hear that. It's just that you and I have known each other since forever. We've always helped each other through these things and it's really weird to think about going it alone."

"Dara will be there."

"I know. You and I just go back a long way, that's all. I'm going to miss you."

"I'll miss you, too."

"Well," said Kate, putting Dara's sparkling clean saddle back on its storage rack. "If we don't get some sleep, I won't be in any shape to go anywhere tomorrow."

They turned off the lights in the tack room and started down the long aisle between the two rows of stalls. Kate smiled. For the first time every stall had a horse in it. Windcroft Stables was full to capacity and her parents were talking about expanding, once the indoor ring was completed and paid for. At least she could go off to Langwald's knowing her parents didn't have any immediate money worries for once.

Instinctively the two girls parted, each seeking out her own horse's stall. Night Owl whinnied softly, and popped his head out over the top of his stall door as Kate approached. Bits of hay stuck out of his mouth at crooked angles. Kate laughed as she scratched behind his ear.

"You can look really ridiculous sometimes, Big Bird." She rubbed underneath his chin, another favorite spot. "Ready for our big month at Langwald's?"

Night Owl butted Kate affectionately with his great head, knocking her slightly off balance. Kate recovered, laughing softly. "Well, I'm glad one of us is. To tell you the truth, I'm a little nervous about the whole thing myself."

"Kate, come here," whispered Jessie as she peered into Time Out's stall. Kate came over and squinted in the dim light. Time Out was standing, eyes half-closed, over her little colt, Tip-Toe, who was curled up at her feet sound asleep.

"Could you really leave them?" Jessie asked. "I mean, if they were yours?"

Kate didn't hesitate. "If it meant getting to the Olympics I could," she whispered back.

Chapter 2

THE rich, golden light of early morning was creeping down the white clapboard buildings of Windcroft Stables when Kate and Jessie headed out to the horses. They slid back the heavy barn door and entered to the sounds of horses anticipating their breakfast—impatient stompings, nervous whinnies, a few knockings of hooves against stall doors.

"Okay, okay, everyone," said Kate. "We're coming."

Night Owl, hearing her voice, let out a piercing whinny.

"I'll fill up the water buckets, if you handle the grain," Kate said to Jessie. "Then we can both do the hay."

The girls set to work and soon the steady noise of horses feeding filled the barn. While Night Owl ate, Kate started to groom him, working first with the hard curry comb, then with the soft body-brush along his sleek, mahogany sides. He was in top shape and the smallest muscles stood out with the slightest movement of his body.

"I might as well get started on Arpeggio," said Jessie.

"I'm sure Dara would really appreciate that," Kate replied. "Better hook him to the cross-tie though."

"Don't worry, I'm not about to wander around in the stall with this big brute," said Jessie, leading Dara's magnificent gray gelding to the grooming area. Arpeggio seemed to nod a haughty "good morning" to all the horses he passed. He didn't exude any of the goofy warmth that Night Owl did. But then, Kate and Dara were very different, too. Dara was methodical, disciplined and logical. Kate was impetuous, moody and brilliant.

Kate started on Night Owl's black mane and tail, brushing them out into silky flows. Much as she hated to admit it, especially since she considered Dara her very best friend next to Jessie, she secretly hoped to prove herself a better rider than Dara. She knew it was Dara's secret drive to beat her, too, so that made it all right somehow.

"We've got some humdinger horse-trials coming up at the end of this month, Big Bird," she whispered to Night Owl as she gently brushed his face. "And, there are going to be some amazing, zillion-dollar horses up there and some terrific riders. We've got to do well, you hear? So you take everything this guy Langwald says seriously, okay?"

Night Owl rubbed his head up and down her sleeve, and Kate kissed his nose. "Sometimes I think you really do understand every word I say."

"Where in the world do you think Dara is?" asked Jessie, when Kate finally led Night Owl out of his stall. She tied him to a lead in the grooming area and began wrapping his legs so he wouldn't injure himself during the van ride north.

"I don't know. She said she'd be here by eight-thirty. It's almost nine now."

They both turned at the sound of a car in the driveway. Kate went to the door of the stables and looked out. The farm was bathed in warm July sun. The hills, falling away on all sides, were green and lush. Her own home sat comfortably in the middle of the land, its wide porches shaded by huge, old maple trees. The main driveway came right by it and a strange car wound its way up.

"It's not Dara," announced Kate. "Must be Mr. Tucker, the van driver." Kate saw her parents, and Pietro Yon, her mother's former riding instructor and longtime family friend, emerge from the house and start toward the barn. Kate's stomach dropped. Soon she would load her horse in the van and drive away from them all for a whole month. She turned back into the barn, feeling queasy and unsure.

"Good morning, Katie May," her dad said warmly, coming up behind her. He patted Night Owl on the rump. "You've certainly got the old boy looking tip-top this morning. How are you feeling?"

"Fine ... just fine," said Kate quietly. She almost wished all these good-byes were over and they were actually on their way. At sixteen years old, she couldn't very well break down and cry like a six-year-old, but that's exactly what she felt like doing.

"We ought to get the horses loaded up soon," said Mr. Wiley. "Mr. Tucker thinks it'll take about four hours to get up there and your mother tells me registration is at two o'clock."

"Let's wait a few more minutes ... for Dara ... before we load," said Kate, knowing her friend would want to put her own horse in the van.

"Good morning, my sweet," said Anne Wiley, limping up on her crutches. "Where's Dara?"

"I'm not sure," Kate replied, getting more and more anxious. "She should have been here half an hour ago."

"Oh, by the way," said Mr. Wiley, a mischievous grin crossing his face as he pulled a tissue-wrapped package from behind his back and handed it to Kate. "This came for you this morning."

Kate looked confused as she peeled back the layers of fragile white paper. Inside lay a single, long-stemmed red rose.

"Oh my gosh!" exclaimed Kate, her breath coming out in a rush. "It's beautiful. But ... who ... what?"

Anne Wiley laughed. "There's a card with it. Open it."

Kate did as she was told, still in shock. No one had ever sent her flowers before. Jessie crowded in closely as Kate read: "Good luck at Langwald's. I'll sure be thinking of you. Pete."

"Oh wow," sighed Jessie. "Is that wonderful or what? Go call him, Kate. Quick."

Kate blushed, and she couldn't decide what to do. Too much was happening all at once.

Just then Mrs. Cooper's Mercedes came charging up the driveway in a cloud of dust. It slid to a stop close enough to cause Arpeggio to prance anxiously for a few steps.

"Gosh, I'm so sorry I'm late," cried Dara, immediately hopping out.

"You're not late, I keep telling you," snapped Mrs. Cooper. "You told me you were leaving at nine-thirty and we're here with minutes to spare."

"But I also told you I had work to finish up, Mother," said Dara. "Do I have time to finish my saddle, Kate? It'll just take me a few minutes."

"We did it for you," said Jessie, coming out of the stables with Dara's saddle in her arms.

"Oh, you guys, I'm so sorry," said Dara despairingly. "Mother just got the brilliant idea this morning that I needed a new formal riding-jacket. Dragged me all the way out to Mitchell's and we had to wait for them to open."

"Hey, don't worry about it," said Kate. "You've certainly covered for us enough times."

"I told you it would be okay," snapped Mrs. Cooper. "Besides, now you'll look wonderful when you get all those ribbons at Langwald's. Oh, you should just see this coat, Anne. Get it out and model it, Dara."

"Mother! For heaven's sake," said Dara, going over to Arpeggio and ignoring her mother's request.

"It's midnight blue," continued Mrs. Cooper to Anne Wiley. "Blue jackets are the latest rage at all the big events. She'll look wonderful in the pictures."

Just then another car started up the drive.

"It's Amory!" cried Jessie. "It's Amory!" Kate

watched Jessie bubble with excitement as the car stopped and her boyfriend got out.

"Hi, Jess," said Amory, and smiled warmly. He put his arm around her shoulders. Jessie beamed up at him. "I thought it was about time I came out to see Time Out's baby. Do you mind?"

"No ... no ... of course not," said Jessie. "Let me just help Dara and Kate get loaded up and on their way. They're off to Vermont today."

"Yeah, I know. Pete told me," said Amory.

Kate smiled inwardly. Pete really did care. She glanced at her watch. She had time to give him a quick call from the new phone in the barn, to thank him for the rose. Kate rushed inside the barn and dialed the number with shaky fingers. Her heart pounded. The rose had said so much; it made her feel so much more sure of their relationship than ever before.

"Pete!" she cried excitedly when he answered the phone.

"Yeah? huh ... what?" came the sleepy reply.

"It's me!"

"Uh ... who?"

"Kate!" she said, her excitement dimming. Okay, so she'd woken him up, but you'd think he'd at least recognize her voice or sound a little more enthusiastic to hear from her or something.

When he only responded with a weak "hi," Kate continued talking. "I just wanted to call and thank you for the rose." She warmed to him all over again just thinking about the beautiful flower he'd sent. "I love it. Thank you ... a lot."

"Sure," he said through a yawn.

"Sorry I woke you up," said Kate, starting to

feel very uncomfortable. This wasn't the intimate "parting is such sweet sorrow" conversation she'd imagined.

"No problem," Pete mumbled. "I'm not really awake anyway."

"Well ... uh, bye, see you in a month," said Kate.

"Bye." Pete yawned.

"Okay, girls," called Mr. Tucker from outside. "Time to get this show on the road."

Kate wandered out feeling shakier and shakier. It was all happening too fast—leaving home, leaving her parents and Jessie, leaving things so weird with Pete. She looked anxiously around as if seeking an escape route from this path that seemed to be leading her away from the safety of her childhood and into independent adulthood. She didn't feel ready for that yet.

"Mom, Dad," she said. "Are you sure you'll be okay without me?"

"Of course, my sweet," said Anne, hugging Kate. "We'll manage just fine."

"July is a slow month for computer programmers," said Mr. Wiley, patting Kate on the back. "So, your mother will get lots of help from me."

"And me," chimed in Jessie.

Kate had sought reassurance, but all she felt was superfluous. They could all get on fine without her. No one needed her. Not even Pete, it seemed.

To calm herself, Kate swore that the first thing she'd do once she got to Langwald's was call Pete again, or at least write him a letter and get things back on track.

Pietro Yon came out of the barn and walked slowly up to Kate. Kate hated to think of him being off in Florida, retired, when she got back. He'd been around since she was born. He was her godfather. He knew everything there was to know about her.

"Well, girlie. You're off into the big world now, eh?" he said kindly as he put his arm around Kate.

Kate just nodded, not trusting herself to speak. There were more tears than words inside her.

"Tommy Langwald's tough. He'll make you or break you. That's his credo. He's trying to sort out who will and who won't make it to the top in this sport. Who's good enough for the Olympic team." He squeezed Kate's shoulder affectionately. "I called him last night and we had a nice chat. He's looking forward to having you this summer."

Kate's head was spinning. She didn't know Mr. Yon knew Langwald personally. What had he said about her? What was Mr. Langwald expecting of her? Would she survive his course? Mr. Yon made it sound worse than she'd ever imagined. Night Owl whinnied through his small window in the van. On his second whinny Kate managed a smile and felt a surge of her old courage. She wasn't really all alone. She had Night Owl. Her smile grew. Yeah ... they'd just have to take old Langwald by storm.

"Kate," said Mr. Yon. "I'll miss you."

"Oh, Mr. Yon," said Kate, flinging her arms around him. "I'll miss you, too. I can't bear to think of you being all that way away."

"I'll be back to check on you from time to time.

Don't you worry," he said, then holding her at
arm's length, added, "Take care of Northern Spy
for me. He and you are all that are left of my
horse world. Find him a good home."

"Of course I will, Pietro," said Kate, hugging her
old friend again. "Maybe I'll find the perfect person at Langwald's."

"Maybe you will, girlie," said Pietro Yon quietly,
walking her over to get in the van. "I certainly
hope so."

Chapter 3

"WHAT a great day!" exclaimed Kate, straining to look out both windows of the van at once. Sunlight splattered the roadway in front of them as they wound higher and higher into the Green Mountains of southern Vermont.

"Don't let it fool you," Mr. Tucker said, grinding down into the lower gears to get the van up the steep rises. "I've been hauling horses up this way for years and I tell you one minute the sun will be shining just as pretty as you please, and the next it'll be pouring rain or dropping hailstones big as golf balls."

"Sounds as changeable as Night Owl." Kate laughed. "He's getting moodier and moodier in his old age and he's only seven. He'll be a certifiable eccentric by the time he's ten."

"You're a little weird yourself," joked Dara. "Maybe he's just taking on your personality."

"Hey, look who's talking," said Kate. "You've

21

hardly said a word since we left and I never exactly thought of you as the quiet, silent type."

"I guess I'm getting a little anxious," admitted Dara. "All the stories we've heard of this place. I have the feeling this Langwald is going to chew us up and spit us out in little pieces."

"So what?" Kate said.

"So, what if I can't put myself back together."

"Is this Miss Confidence herself I'm listening to?" teased Kate.

"That's Mother," said Dara. "Not me. It was her idea for me to go to Langwald's in the first place."

Kate looked at Dara in surprise. "But I thought you were really gung ho to go."

"Oh, I don't know, Kate. I really don't," Dara said, then turned her attention to the mountains outside.

"Does this strange mood you're in have anything to do with Doug, by any chance?" asked Kate after a few minutes of silence.

Dara studied Kate for a second. "You're not supposed to know me that well yet."

"Hey, give me a break," said Kate. "You moved up from Pennsylvania five months ago, right?"

"Yes."

"And we go to the same school, and spend all our free time at my stables, right?"

"Yeah," agreed Dara.

"Okay, so I think that's plenty of time to get to know each other." Kate turned so she could look Dara straight in the face. "Now let's hear it. What's going on with Doug?"

Dara slumped back in her seat. The mid-July heat had frizzed her hair. She looked as beautiful as ever, but for the first time since she'd known her, Dara looked vulnerable to Kate.

"It's kind of weird," Dara began. "I mean ... I really like him. He's kind and cares a lot. All that good stuff. I mean ... we have a great time together." She paused and nervously wound a curl around her finger. "But he wants every second of my time. That is, every second when *he's* not busy. He just doesn't seem to understand that my whole life can't be devoted to him."

"Do you wish it could?" asked Kate.

"Wow, are you in training to be a lawyer, or what!" Dara laughed. Then she added, "Sometimes I think it would be a lot easier not to be pulled in all these directions."

"Meaning?"

"I don't know." Dara ran her fingers nervously through her hair. "I'm just going to throw myself into this whole Langwald thing and see what happens."

"Cooper, you're not making much sense," Kate said.

"It's because nothing's clear to me," Dara answered. She smiled warmly at Kate. "Don't worry, I'll let you know when it is."

"Okay," Kate said. "I'll be here."

"What about you and Pete?" Dara asked. "Jessie told me about the rose."

"Oh my gosh!" exclaimed Kate, looking around frantically. "I forgot it! I left it at home."

"Uh-huh," Dara said. "Zer must be zee good reason for dis, Miz Wiley. Yez, yez. In my learned opinion, as professor of zee psychology, I would say dis is meaning you vant to leave dis Pete behind, too. Ya. Am I correct being?"

Kate laughed. "Aren't you taking your German a little too seriously?" she teased.

Dara was laughing too hard to answer.

"You know, I really care for Pete ... a lot," Kate said, getting serious. She was upset about forgetting the rose. "But maybe the relationship is too new. I don't know. Maybe it's because he's the first boy I've ever really cared about like in boyfriend-girlfriend. But I just can't get a handle on it. Everything seemed so perfect and then when I called him this morning he sounded really weird. Okay, so I woke him up, but he didn't sound very excited about hearing from me, and we're not going to see each other for a whole month." Kate stared out the window for a moment. "Maybe I expect too much."

"You do set pretty outrageous goals, Kate," Dara said. "Of course, that's why you get so far, too."

"Do you think I'm pushing things too much with Pete?" Kate asked.

"Naw. Not really. Pete's just laid back. You're always two steps ahead of him, but I don't think that bothers him. He's cool."

"Yeah, I guess he can handle me." Kate laughed.

"If anyone can, he can," agreed Dara.

"Well girls, we've officially entered the Green Mountain National Forest," announced Mr. Tucker over the roar of the engine. "Passed the sign right back there."

The girls peered around, taking it all in. There

were signs for hiking trails and picnic tables and scenic views.

"Wouldn't it be great to get out for awhile?" exclaimed Kate.

"Would it ever," Dara agreed. "My whole body is stiff."

"And I know how much Night Owl hates being cooped up in the van for a long time. Since his and Arpeggio's legs are taped for traveling, we can't ride them but we could let them graze while we take a hike." Kate turned to the driver. "What do you say, Mr. Tucker? How about a break for lunch? Mother packed a picnic big enough for at least eight people."

"But I thought you girls had to be at Langwald's by two o'clock," replied Mr. Tucker.

"That's just when registration begins," said Kate. "It probably goes on all afternoon. They wouldn't have anything else scheduled, I'm sure."

"I don't know," said Dara doubtfully. "From what I hear, this Langwald isn't one for idle moments."

Kate hesitated.

"But it's such a beautiful day," said Dara. "We could enjoy it for just a little while."

"Agreed!" said Kate.

Mr. Tucker had barely maneuvered the big van off the road when the two girls jumped out.

"This is perfect," Dara said, looking around. They had the small picnic area to themselves. There were three tables situated alongside a creek that tumbled down the mountain with a noisy gurgle. A hiking trail started on its far side and disappeared into the bank of trees beyond.

"It's too wonderful," Kate said, opening the large side door to the van. Dara and Mr. Tucker helped her pull out the ramp and lock it into place.

"I hope you girls know what you're doing," Mr. Tucker said doubtfully. "I feel kind of responsible for you."

"Don't worry, Mr. Tucker," said Kate. "The sign says it's only one mile to the top of Old Baldy. Sounds like a nice place to eat lunch. We'll only be gone about an hour."

"Okay, I guess that sounds reasonable. I'll take care of the horses," he said.

In two seconds flat, the girls had their horses out and tied to a tree in some tall grass. Night Owl pranced around excitedly. "No, Night Owl, I can't take you riding with your legs all bandaged. Just relax and enjoy the grass." Kate patted her horse, while Dara had a similar conversation with Arpeggio.

The only thing they had to carry their picnic in was Dara's pocketbook. She dumped all her stuff out on the shelf in the horse van, and refilled her bag with sandwiches and apples. They left the rest of the goodies for Mr. Tucker.

"Let's go," said Kate.

"See you in about an hour, Mr. Tucker," called Dara, as she and Kate took off on the hiking trail.

"Keep an eye on the weather, girls," shouted Mr. Tucker, picking up a fat sandwich.

The trail up the mountain was steep and rocky, but the girls hardly noticed. The sun soaked through their shirts and the blue sky overhead lured them on.

"It's kind of neat to be out in the world all on our own, isn't it?" asked Dara.

"Yeah," answered Kate. "No one in the whole world knows where we are."

"Except Mr. Tucker."

"He doesn't count right now," Kate said. "I want to enjoy this feeling of having complete control over my own life."

"I agree," said Dara. "In fact, wouldn't it be fun to just keep hiking and hiking, day after day, over these mountains, camping out at night, totally independent."

"It sure would," agreed Kate. "But it would be more fun if we had the horses on a camping trip."

"Wow," said Dara. "Check out this view. We're really high up. It even feels colder up here."

"It does," agreed Kate, stopping and resting against a tree. "I'm starving. Let's eat."

Dara sat next to Kate on the rock ledge overlooking the surrounding mountains and the valley far below. She opened her pocketbook and dished out the goodies.

"Tuna fish!" said Kate, and bit into her sandwich. "My favorite. Good old Mom." The taste of the tuna fish reminded her of home and Kate felt filled again with loss at being so far away. Langwald's loomed threateningly.

"Jessie would like it up here," Dara said, cutting up an apple with her Swiss army knife. She handed Kate a piece.

"She sure would," said Kate, feeling more and more homesick. "I wish she'd come with us."

"Me, too," said Dara. "But Jessie knows what's

best for her. She's really got a handle on things these days."

"That's for sure."

"I admire her for it." Dara sighed and chomped into her apple. "She makes balancing home, horses and boyfriends look so easy."

"Look at those clouds over there," said Kate. "Hanging around the top of that peak."

"Weird, huh? The rest of the sky's completely clear."

"It looks like it's pouring rain on top of that mountain."

"While it's still sunny in the valley below."

"Kind of like life, isn't it?" said Kate after a few minutes of staring at the contrasting scene before them.

"Is it?" Dara responded, confused.

"Yeah," said Kate, sitting up straight. "Some people's lives are like the valley down there—safe and protected with not too many ups and downs. While others' are like this range of mountains— all up and down, going from one extreme to the other."

"I'm more of the valley-type, I think," said Dara.

"I wish I were," Kate said. "Sometimes I get worn out from all the extremes."

"And I wish my life had more peaks," said Dara. "You can see farther from the peaks than you can tucked away in a valley."

Kate laughed. "Listen to us. We sound like a couple of ancient philosophers."

"Actually, it's probably oxygen deprivation from being up so high. Our minds are turning to mush."

Dara laughed. She stood up and brushed the dirt off her jeans. "I think we should head back."

"I guess so. It's just so peaceful up here," said Kate.

"I thought you just said the peaks were so extreme," Dara teased.

"I did. I'm extremely peaceful right now," Kate shot back, and grinned broadly.

"You're getting more and more like Night Owl every day." Dara laughed. "Totally weird!"

"It's getting chilly, isn't it?" said Kate, as she stood up and stretched.

"Yeah, and look at those black clouds we were admiring a few minutes ago," added Dara. "Looks like they're coming for a visit, doesn't it?"

"We better burn this trail up," Kate said, breaking into a jog.

They ran when they could, but most of the time the rocky trail forced them to walk. The wind blew stronger and stronger and by the time they were halfway back, the first raindrops fell—big, heavy raindrops that stung when they landed.

"Oh, no, we're going to get soaked," shouted Dara over the mounting storm. "Make sure you stay right behind me."

As the rain got so heavy that they could barely see in front of themselves, Kate caught up with Dara and grabbed her hand. They walked slowly down the rain-slicked trail, the trees and brush on either side whipping wildly back and forth. Kate shivered from the cold. The storm followed them all the way back to the clearing where the van was parked. Mr. Tucker had his slicker on and was pacing anxiously back and forth beside it. He rushed up to greet them.

"Wow, were you ever right about this weather, Mr. Tucker!" Kate said, out of breath, when the three of them were finally in the safety of the van. "Pretty wild stuff."

"Well, you young ladies look like drowned rats, but your horses are nice and dry. I took care of them for you," Mr. Tucker said as he gunned the engine.

"We may look like we drowned but we survived that storm, so I expect we can survive anything old Langwald can throw at us," Dara said.

"You bet!" cried Kate, pushing her soggy hair back from her face. "Onward to Langwald's."

"Onward!" shouted Dara. And even Mr. Tucker laughed.

Chapter 4

"FORTY-EIGHT bottles of beer on the wall, forty-eight bottles of beer," Kate sang.

"No!" Dara protested and laughed. "No! We just did forty-eight. We're down to forty-seven."

"No way. It's either forty-eight or forty-nine."

"I guess we'll just have to start over," said Dara.

Kate groaned dramatically and fell over on the van seat. "No ... please. Fine. I agree to forty-seven. Anything. Just don't start over. I'm sick to death of this song."

"Me, too," Dara said.

"Then why, may I ask, are we still singing it?"

"Have you got any other brilliant suggestions on how to keep ourselves from going stark-raving mad in here?"

"Hang on, girls," broke in Mr. Tucker. "We're getting close to Langwald's. The fences have started."

Kate and Dara looked out the windows. The mountains were behind them, still in view, but the van was moving along the floor of the valley now. Dark-colored, beautifully maintained plank fencing ran along both sides of the narrow country road. The fields within were just as impeccable. The girls took it all in.

"Gosh," Dara said, letting her breath out finally in a rush. "Take a look at those horses."

"Wow! They're really something. Look at that bay." Kate pointed to a large, stunning, shiny brown horse with a black mane and tail. "Looks like Night Owl."

"Yeah, if the good fairy touched him a couple of times with her magic wand," joked Dara.

"Hey, just you wait till the trials," said Kate. "Night Owl's going to knock 'em dead."

The barns, painted in the same dark creosote as the fences and sporting red roofs, came into view. A white Vermont farmhouse sat surrounded by the barns, giving the farm a unified look. Hills rose up behind the buildings, then dropped into lush, groomed pastures that rolled easily down to a broad river.

"Oh my gosh!" Dara exclaimed suddenly. "Look at me! My jeans are still damp. And my shoes are trashed."

"Quick, give me your brush!" Kate said, starting to undo her long, tangled, still damp braid. "We can't show up looking like this."

"My brush!" cried Dara. "Oh no! It's in the back of the van with all my makeup. I dumped it out of my pocketbook before I packed our lunch."

"Ah well, at least Arpeggio will look handsome."

"Don't joke," Dara said. "He's probably eaten my mascara."

"Well, I never heard of a horse dying from mascara poisoning." Kate giggled.

"I might die from lack of mascara," moaned Dara, running her hands through her hair and trying to bring a bit of order to it.

"Look," said Kate reassuringly. "We'll unload the horses, get them settled, then hit the showers. We'll be right as rain in no time."

"I would have appreciated a different choice of words." Dara laughed.

The van slowed down and both girls forgot about their disheveled appearances for a moment as they stared around.

"Here we are," said Mr. Tucker, swinging the van into the long straight driveway underneath the arch-shaped sign that said LANGWALD'S.

"Gosh," said Kate, almost in a whisper. "It's so beautiful around here, you'd think he'd have found a better name for this place."

"Yeah, like Riverside Acres," added Dara, staring. "Or Rolling Meadows."

"Even Black Fence Farm," said Kate with a nervous giggle. Her heart was in her mouth. So this was the famous Langwald's. Her home for the next month. Her riding was going to be judged here like it had never been judged before in her life. She swallowed hard. Her throat felt dry and scratchy.

"I've got to head on back," said Mr. Tucker, "so let's get these animals on out as quickly as possible."

Kate looked at him, feeling desperation rising

inside. She couldn't believe he was just going to dump them there. Not that she felt particularly close to him or anything, but he was their last link to home and it made her want to hold on. But Mr. Tucker was out of the truck and soon was leading Night Owl out. The horse had obviously been asleep. Both ears flopped out to the sides and he blinked his great brown eyes against the harsh sun. Kate took the lead shank from Mr. Tucker and patted Night Owl's neck.

"Well, Big Bird, we're here," she whispered into his soft, warm ear.

"The makeup's history," said Dara, leading Arpeggio out. "Stomped to bits."

They tied the horses to a nearby fencepost, then began unloading their saddles and suitcases.

"I take it you're Kate Wiley from Connecticut."

Kate whirled around. A large, powerfully built man in riding clothes and with a short, clipped haircut was bearing down on them. Kate felt immediately pleased that he knew who she was.

"Yes," she said, unable to stick out her hand as her arms were full of saddle. She tried to flick her half-undone braid to her back but it plopped heavily on her shoulder, stringy and damp.

"Then you can put that saddle straight up on your horse and join the others in the ring," he said. "Class started ten minutes ago."

"Class!" said Kate, bewildered. "I thought we were supposed to register."

"Registration was at two o'clock." His eyes were dark and intense as he spoke. "It is now three-thirty."

"Oh ... well ... yes," babbled Kate. "We're sorry, of course. It's just that it was such a beautiful day that we stopped to have a picnic in the Green Mountains."

The dark eyes bored into her. "I shall assume you have come here to work. Getting to the Olympics is no picnic. Do you understand?"

"Yes ... yes ... certainly," stammered Kate.

"Then saddle up. Both of you. And get into the ring."

"Do I have time to run a brush over my horse?"

"I'm not concerned with what your horse looks like," the man snapped, "but how he moves, and how you make him move. I'll see you in the ring."

Just then a short, plump girl in an oversized T-shirt ran up. She smiled warmly from behind the man's back and winked at them.

"Excuse me," she said, addressing the man. "But Dr. Andrews wants you in the barn. He said it was about Ellie."

Kate saw a flash of concern, even sadness, wash over the man's face. He started to turn away, then swung around again. "By the way, I'm Tommy Langwald. *Mr.* Langwald."

Kate and Dara stood watching him walk away, too stunned to move.

"And I'm Casey O'Connell," said the chubby girl, mocking Mr. Langwald's deep voice. She laughed.

Kate felt herself relax a bit. She smiled back at Casey. "I'm Kate Wiley."

"And I'm Dara Cooper," Dara chimed in.

"Well, I've got to get back to the ring," said Casey cheerfully. "Or old Fangwald might have me for supper."

Kate and Dara laughed.

"Fangwald, that's good," said Dara.

"Pretty appropriate, if you ask me," added Kate.

"Okay girls, I'm off," called Mr. Tucker from the cabin of the van. Kate felt her eyes fill with tears. If only she could pack herself and Night Owl back up in that van and go home. They'd be there by dark; all safe and warm at Windcroft.

"Let's get these saddles on," said Dara calmly. "And get to the ring before we're in any more trouble."

The girls waved to Mr. Tucker, then quickly got their horses tacked up. They rummaged around in their luggage and found their boots and hard hats and soon were following Casey's path to the ring.

Chapter 5

NIGHT OWL pricked up his ears as they approached the riding ring. Kate's heart sank. There were seven horses, beautifully groomed, walking calmly along the rail. The riders were all kids, both boys and girls, about her age, but their jodhpurs were spotless and their boots shiny. Even Dara had managed to tuck her hair into her hat and find her best boots. Kate knew she looked like a complete wreck with her muddy jeans and stringy hair. She could feel the stares. But she lifted her chin, shortened her reins slightly to let Night Owl know they were at work, not play, and entered the ring as if it were the most important event of her life—shoulders squared, heels down, weight deep in the saddle. Tommy Langwald strode in just then, too.

"Please, Night Owl," prayed Kate. "Don't fail me now."

"All right, class," he boomed. "Sorry about the delay."

Kate felt her cheeks redden.

"Where were we?" he continued. "Ah yes, I wanted to get an overall view of you and your horses so I know what I'm working with for the next month. So, if you would just continue at a nice brisk walk, please. I will then ask you to trot, canter, halt—in that order—then we'll reverse directions. Thank you."

Whew, thought Kate, relaxing a bit. That sounds easy enough.

"I think you could apply a bit more pressure with those legs, Miss Wiley," barked Langwald. "Your horse seems a bit sluggish in the hindquarters."

Kate did as she was told. Night Owl broke into a trot.

"Please, Miss Wiley, I did say a walk."

Yeah, thought Kate angrily, you also said to apply more pressure. Any horse worth his oats knows that means to get a move on. She reined Night Owl back down into a walk.

"The message from the legs must be countered by a subtle message from the hands," Mr. Langwald explained to the class, "in order for you to control the pace absolutely. Now, let's see what the trot looks like."

Kate squeezed imperceptibly with her legs and tightened the reins ever so slightly. Night Owl responded instantly and Kate smiled. Take that, Fangwald, she thought.

"Collect that trot, Miss Wiley," he called after her. "Try to round him out with your back and legs."

The poor horse has been in a van all morning,

Kate fumed silently. So he's not in the best mood. Would you be?

Kate knew if she got tense, Night Owl would get cross signals from her and really screw up, so she willed herself to remain calm and did as she was told. Night Owl responded with a composed, springy trot.

"Better," Langwald noted. Out of the corner of her eye Kate could see him turning his attention to Dara. She and Arpeggio looked magnificent. Dara sat easily astride the big gray. His neck was arch-shaped, his mouth quiet, his movements smooth as honey. Kate wondered what Langwald would find wrong there. He was obviously out to make them all feel like complete losers this first day.

"Not bad, Miss Cooper," he said.

Not bad! thought Kate with a twinge of jealousy. How does Dara rate a "not bad" and all I get is a rough time?

While Langwald was involved on the other side of the ring, Kate took the opportunity to sneak looks at the other students. There were four boys and five girls, and horses of all shapes and colorings. One horse was positively ugly, a large pinto whose neck seemed too long for his short body. The boy astride him sat easily and relaxed. Kate smiled at Casey as their gazes met. Too bad Casey isn't about ten pounds lighter, Kate mused as she watched the chubby girl. She sat well on her little black mare, but the extra weight ruined the whole sleek line of horse and rider as one.

Kate continued her assessment of the others, wondering, at the same time, what they were

thinking about her. The girl right in front of her
was an excellent rider and her large chestnut
horse moved nicely, but something about them
looked weird to Kate. The horse was doing his
thing, the girl was doing hers; their bodies were
in the same place, but their minds obviously
weren't. They weren't connecting. Maybe the girl
was just having a bad day, like Night Owl sometimes had. Some days you couldn't ask for a more
perfect horse, others he had a mind of his own.
She was hoping the month at Langwald's would
smooth him out.

Langwald put them through the basic paces for
another half hour or so, then called them into the
center of the ring.

"Now then, I want to observe you one at a time.
Mr...." Langwald hesitated. "Trevor Williams, isn't
it?"

The boy on the ugly pinto nodded.

"Well then, Mr. Williams. You will go first. I
want a working trot down the center of the ring
to the end, track right, circle, halt, then rein back
five steps.... I hope you're all listening, because
I'm only going to say this once. Walk for two
strides, half halt, extended trot for five strides,
working trot back up here, full halt for three
seconds."

Kate watched the pinto with disbelief. The minute Trevor began working him, the horse was
transformed. His awkward body became graceful
and supple. His transitions between gaits were
barely noticeable, and his neck, which had seemed
too long, looked perfect now in its arch-shape.

Trevor controlled him easily with imperceptible signals from his hands, legs shifting weight.

"Watch those hands," said Langwald when Trevor reined in. "They're a bit high."

Casey went next.

"Can you feel how that extra weight throws you off?" Langwald called after her. Kate felt bad for Casey. Imagine having someone give you a rough time about your weight right in front of all these people. This Langwald is inhuman, she thought.

"Okay," said Langwald, when Casey trotted up to the back of the line. "Caroline Randolph. You're next."

The girl who'd been warming up in front of Kate turned her horse to the center of the ring and began the routine. Again Kate was impressed with the performance, but still felt there was something essential lacking. Langwald didn't even look up from his note-taking when Caroline finished.

Kate assessed each performance from atop Night Owl as horse after horse was put to the test. Finally it was her turn. She felt confident. Yes, there were some good riders here and yes, there were some spectacular horses, but she and Night Owl knew what they were doing. She began to trot down the ring. Night Owl felt a little rough. She shifted her weight to get him further back on his haunches. By the time they were ready for the half halt, he was moving smoothly. The rest of the exercise went without a hitch. Kate patted his neck when they finished.

"It's not a good idea to issue undeserved reward," said Langwald.

Kate felt like she'd been punched in the stom-

ach. Undeserved reward! They'd done a good job.
Okay, so Night Owl was a little sluggish at first
because he'd been standing around for fifteen
minutes waiting his turn. What did Langwald
expect?

"Okay class, there's a lot of work to be done if
you're going to be ready for the horse trials in
four weeks." It seemed to Kate as if he were
looking directly at her. She squirmed uncomfort-
ably. Night Owl took two steps forward. "Miss
Wiley, control your mount please," snapped
Langwald. Kate felt her face go bright red as she
exerted a slight backward pressure on the reins
and Night Owl reversed into his place.

"As I was saying, there's a lot of work to be
done," Langwald continued. "I expect you to take
it seriously. Not only the work in the ring, but the
work around the stables and farm. There's a bulletin board next to the tack room on which you'll
find a list of chores to be done. Your names are
posted next to each. Dinner is at six o'clock sharp.
Lights out at ten. You will have one wake-up call
at six A.M. If any of this doesn't suit someone for
whatever reason, please feel free to pack up your
horse and go home. My job here is to improve
your abilities as eventers, and ..." He paused
here and let his eye run down the line of riders. "I
assure you I will."

"Can you believe that guy?" asked Kate as she
and Night Owl fell in beside Dara and Arpeggio.
They filtered out of the ring with the others.

"Yeah, he's a toughie," Dara said.

"I wonder what he's trying to prove."

"I think he genuinely wants to make us better riders," said Dara. "He's tough, but he gets results."

"Whose side are you on, anyway?" Kate asked. "The guy's a regular marine sergeant."

"It's not a question of sides," explained Dara. "We came up here to improve our riding, right?"

"Right."

"I think Langwald can do it, although I agree he could be a little less bloodthirsty."

"A little less bloodthirsty!" cried Kate. "He makes Rambo look like Snow White."

Dara laughed. "Oh Kate, you're always so dramatic. Let's go get these poor beasties comfortable in their new home, then check out our work assignments."

Each horse's name had been written on a temporary sign over his stall door. Kate led Night Owl into his and let out a deep sigh.

"I know that sigh," said a voice from the next stall. "It's the 'I'd-like-to-murder-Tommy-Langwald sigh.'"

Kate could see Casey's face peeking through the rails between the stalls. She laughed. "You've got that right."

"This is my second summer of listening to this guy," continued Casey. "I . . ."

"You mean you came back for more abuse?" Kate interrupted with surprise.

"Not by choice, I tell you," Casey replied. "My parents said I could go here or a fat farm. But either way, I have to lose fifteen pounds."

"Casey, that's terrible."

"Well, you've got to admit, this place is better than a fat farm."

"What a horrible name. Fat farm."

"It's kind of hard to call it anything else. Pleasantly plump estate, maybe? Or chub club."

Kate giggled. "How can you still have a sense of humor after old Fangwald chewed you out like that?"

"Actually, I'm just about to burst into tears," said Casey and Kate couldn't tell if she was serious or still joking. "But, I think I'll have a donut instead. Want one?" A hand with a crumpled brown bag came through the rails. Night Owl sniffed at it curiously.

"No thanks," said Kate, pushing Night Owl's nose back toward the hayrack. "Are donuts part of your diet?"

Casey laughed. "Nope. I'm not starting that until tomorrow. It won't take you long to learn that one of my most winning points is that I have absolutely no discipline whatsoever. A regular hedonist. So, if you don't want the last donut, I'll just dig into it myself."

Kate didn't feel quite so lost with Casey next door. She set about untacking Night Owl. He munched contentedly at his hay and occasionally flicked a fly off his back with his tail.

"Oh Casey, the Robber Baron is ready whenever you are."

Kate glanced out of the stall to the voice with its slow Southern accent. It was Caroline, her slender figure sporting the very latest in chic riding gear, her brown, beautifully cut hair swinging loose to her shoulders.

"Sure, Caroline. I'll get right on it," said Casey pleasantly.

"Did you ride Caroline's horse today?" asked Kate, when Caroline had sauntered away.

"No," Casey answered. "I'm grooming him."

"Why?" Kate said with surprise.

"Because," began Casey, mimicking Caroline's accent. "Miss Caroline Randolph of Virginia doesn't groom her horse, or polish her boots, or saddlesoap her saddle. I do."

"For heaven's sakes, why?" asked Kate.

"Because she doesn't like to and I need the money," said Casey. "Now, before you go telling me how bad that is, let's go check out our duties this week. I'll show you where the tack room is."

Kate patted Night Owl's neck. "This place is more weird than I thought it was going to be," she whispered in his ear. Her stomach felt queasy with homesickness and it took all her willpower to leave her horse, but she dutifully gathered up her saddle and bridle and followed Casey down the aisle. The tack room was near the center of the barn where the two long arms of the stable met. Every inch of the barn was spotless and in absolute order. Kate paused in front of the bulletin board. The list of jobs read like a battle plan. It seemed like Langwald wanted them to do all but lick the floors clean.

"There you are," said Casey, pointing to Kate's name halfway down the list. "Lucky you."

"Why?" asked Kate.

"You get to muck out the stalls."

"Great. Really lucky."

"With—Tum Ta Ta Taaaa—Trevor Williams," joked Casey.

Kate giggled. "Are you ever serious?"

"Yes, every time I step on the scales. And," she continued, "every time I think of Trevor Williams."

"Your kind of guy, huh?" teased Kate.

"Without a doubt," sighed Casey, and again it was hard for Kate to assess if Casey was joking or not.

"What's my job?" asked Dara, coming up to join them. "Have you ever seen such an organized barn before? Wow, I've just had the tour. You could be blind and still find everything. I love it."

"You would," Kate said, then turning to Casey, she explained. "Everyone at school thinks Dara was a computer in her former life. She's so organized and disciplined, she's positively inhuman."

"I'm not that bad," said Dara with a laugh.

"You'll do fine here, if you are," said Casey. "In case you haven't guessed, discipline and organization are Fangwald's middle names. Thomas Discipline Organization Fangwald. Family names from Transylvania, you see."

Dara and Kate both laughed.

"This is interesting. Look at my job," said Dara after consulting the list. "Double check fire emergency equipment. Each stall must have a bucket of water, a towel and a lead shank outside the door at all times."

"Geez. The guy's paranoid, too," said Kate.

"I don't know," said Dara. "Imagine if this place did catch on fire and you couldn't find a lead shank. Or a horse panicked and you didn't have something to blindfold him with."

"Dara, when was the last time you heard of a barn burning down?" Kate asked with slight annoyance in her tone. Dara actually seemed to be enjoying this military routine.

"Yeah, I know, but you'd like to be prepared if it did, wouldn't you?"

Kate sighed. "Someday, Dara, you are going to organize yourself out of existence."

"Excuse me," came a pleasant voice. "Aren't you Kate Wiley?"

"Y—Yes," stammered Kate.

"We seem to be work partners. I just wondered if you'd like to get started now since we missed the morning chores."

"Oh, right. You're Trevor, aren't you?" Kate asked, feeling her cheeks go red-hot. He had the most amazing blue eyes she'd ever seen—all sparkly and full of fun. "Sure, might as well get going. Have you met Dara Cooper and Casey O'Connell?"

Trevor bowed slightly at the waist to each girl. Casey looked like she was about to pass out from excitement. Kate giggled, and followed Trevor down the aisle.

"How are we going to muck out stalls with the horses in them?" asked Kate.

"Mr. Langwald explained all that after lunch. In the afternoon, we freshen up the stalls at this end first because the horses are out in the paddocks, then the others later when we put our horses out," said Trevor. "How come you arrived so late anyway?"

Kate felt guilty again about missing registration. "Uh ... well ... my friend, Dara, and I hiked up a mountain for a picnic lunch and sort of forgot about the time."

"It was a beautiful day, wasn't it?" Trevor opened the door to a large room that had pitchforks and shovels and buckets and sponges all neatly arranged along the walls. He selected two pitchforks and handed one to Kate. "My favorite is riding by the light of the full moon."

"Wow! I've never done that before! It sounds amazing!"

"The moon will be full soon. Maybe we could go then?"

Kate felt a shiver of excitement run through her. What an adventure that would be, she thought.

Trevor pushed the wheelbarrow up to the first stall. He and Kate began shoveling muck into it, and they worked comfortably, side by side. Kate knew she must look terrible by now with bits and pieces of hay in her tangled hair and sweat running down her face, but it felt nice to be working with Trevor. He was easy to be around.

"I certainly never knew mucking out stalls could be so much fun," Trevor said and laughed. "I think I have you to thank for this, Miss Wiley."

Kate giggled and tossed more muck in the barrow. "And I, Mr. Williams, must thank you for a delightful time."

"We'll have to do this again sometime," Trevor said with fake solemnity.

"Yeah, in about an hour at the other end of the barn," Kate deadpanned.

"Oh woe, you obviously don't have the soul of a true romantic," said Trevor with mock despair.

"Smelly hay and horse muffins do not inspire romance," said Kate, carrying out the charade.

"Let's talk white sand beaches and picnics at sunset."

"And moonlit rides," said Trevor.

Kate didn't answer. She felt she'd somehow lost control of the conversation and didn't know how to get it back.

Finally the wheelbarrow was full. They pushed it out behind the barn and dumped it onto the huge compost pile, then leaned on their pitchforks to rest for a second.

"Do you have a special boyfriend?" asked Trevor, his friendly blue eyes locked on her face. Kate didn't know where to look, so she looked around, at everything and nothing at once.

"Yes ... no ... I mean ..." She began giggling nervously. "I mean there is someone but he's not into horses, so we don't get much time together."

Thinking of Pete made Kate miss him. Why had she told Trevor that Pete wasn't into horses? Okay, maybe he didn't know a whole lot about them but he was always eager to be with her and Night Owl. He helped out where he could. Maybe I should write to him—tonight, she thought. And apologize for waking him up or something. Try to get things back to normal.

When she looked back at Trevor, he was still staring intently at her.

Chapter 6

"WELL, I definitely think old Fangwald should hand out medals today," said Kate, pulling her cotton nightgown over her head and tossing it onto her bed.

"Hmm ... uggghhh," mumbled Dara from beneath her covers.

"You ask why," teased Kate. "Because ... because we have survived two weeks in this place. No bones broken. No deaths from overwork." she pulled on a T-shirt. "Okay, maybe a few minds lost, a few bruised egos, things like that ..."

"Turn off the sun," moaned Dara. "I'm trying to sleep."

"If you don't get out of bed," Kate said, "you might well be our first casualty. Just imagine what Fangwald will do to you if you miss his infamous eight A.M. workout."

"I don't care," said Dara, pulling her pillow over her head. "I'm exhausted. I've never worked so hard in my life."

"Writing letters to Doug," said Kate. "What time did you turn off the light last night, huh?"

"Okay, okay, I got a bit carried away," Dara said. "I miss my boyfriend. Is that such a big crime?"

"No, but having your flashlight on an hour and a half after 'lights out' might just be your downfall," continued Kate, zipping up her slick-fitting jodhpurs. No jeans allowed at Langwald's; at least not for classes.

"You're just jealous," snapped Dara.

"Uh-oh, your phone call to Doug didn't go too well yesterday, I take it?" Kate said, a little more gently.

Dara sat up suddenly. "If you must know, it was the pits."

"Gosh, Dara, I'm really sorry. What happened? You want to talk about it?"

"Oh ... I don't know," sighed Dara. "It's the same old story. He just doesn't seem to understand that my riding can be anywhere near as important as his tennis." Dara flopped back on her bed. "You know, I really envy you having Trevor."

"Having Trevor! I don't 'have' anyone," Kate said indignantly.

"Well, you're the only one who doesn't know it," said Dara. "Haven't you noticed that wherever you are, he is?"

"No ... I mean, we're friends and we've gotten stuck together on work detail a couple of times." Kate could hardly hear herself over her pounding heart.

"All I'm saying, Kate Wiley," continued Dara, "is

be thankful you've got a boyfriend who's into horses. It makes things a lot easier."

"He's not my boyfriend," Kate protested.

Dara wasn't listening though. Her head was back under her pillow and the covers were pulled up under her chin. Kate flopped down on her bed feeling utterly confused, and for a few minutes her gaze roamed aimlessly around the cheery little room. The curtains were blue chintz and the furniture, country pine—two beds, two dressers, a desk and chair, and a rocking chair. There were several framed photographs of horses on the walls. Kate's favorite was the one called Elsinore of Bodiam. She had never heard such a romantic name before, or seen such a magnificent horse. It was a palomino with a pale blond coat and an almost white tail and mane, just the sort of horse she'd always imagined a knight in shining armor to ride up on and steal her away to his castle. She giggled at her fantasy, realized she was feeling better, so she gave Dara one last wake-up shake, and ran down to breakfast.

"Kate, I saved you a seat," Trevor called, indicating the chair next to his at the long table where all the students sat.

After what Dara had said, Kate felt embarrassed even to look at Trevor. But she did, and then couldn't help noticing how good looking he really was. His whole face lit up when he smiled. Was it possible that he really liked her? Could she ever think of him as more than a friend? What about Pete? He hadn't bothered to contact her at all since she'd arrived, but then she'd never written to him either. There wasn't time, she argued with herself. Every night she hit the pillow and fell asleep instantly, completely exhausted. There wasn't time up here to think of anything but horses and riding and the endless list of tasks Langwald insisted on to keep his precious farm superorganized.

"Good morning, Trevor," Kate said, and sat down next to him. He pushed the raisin bran—her favorite cereal—over to her. "Thanks." But she felt too keyed up to eat. She swallowed a couple of bites, then pushed her bowl away.

"I want to get in a few minutes with Night Owl before class today," she said to Trevor. "Try to loosen him up a bit before the jumping."

"Great," said Trevor. "Paint-Patch could use the extra time, too. I'll join you."

Kate had never felt so torn. It would be wonderful to have Trevor there. They could help each other like they always did, but she didn't feel in control of the situation. Her conversation with Dara had really thrown her into a major state of confusion.

"I—I really need to be alone," stammered Kate. "Langwald keeps giving Night Owl and me such a rough time. I've got to try to figure out what's wrong and fix it."

"Sure," said Trevor, pouring himself another bowl of cereal. "I can understand that." He smiled at her. "Good luck. See you later."

"Yeah," said Kate, searching his face for something even she couldn't define. "See you."

Kate dashed out the door and almost ran into Langwald, head down, walking slowly back to the house from his private barns.

"Good morning, Mr. Langwald," she called out, then noticed Dr. Andrews heading out of the barn to his van.

"Hmm," he replied absentmindedly, not looking up.

Kate turned and watched him walk up the steps to the house. He seemed very sad and, for the first time, he seemed human to Kate. She rushed on to the stables. Langwald had promised them a superintensive jumping lesson this morning. Night Owl loved to jump and Kate wanted him to be really warmed up and ready for it.

"Hello gorgeous," she said, slipping into the horse's stall. Night Owl whinnied his hello, then eagerly took the piece of apple she offered. She rubbed his soft nose and ears. "You've got to jump like a champ today. Okay? I'm determined to have Langwald say one nice thing about us."

Night Owl nudged her with his nose, searching for more apple. Kate teased him for a while, then slipped him the second piece.

"Okay, let me get my chores done and I'll be right back," she said, kissing his cheek. "Don't go away now, you hear?"

Night Own nickered softly, and the sound filled her with joy.

Kate couldn't believe the task she'd been given this week. She had to check every door and window in the stables to be certain they worked easily on their hinges. If not, she had to oil them. She shook her head at the bizarre task as she went from stall to stall, testing the doors. When one squeaked or ground on itself, she blasted it with her oil can. Langwald insisted she do this every day.

"Sometimes I think he tries to see just how weird he can make his orders and still have us follow them," mumbled Kate as she worked her way down the barn.

Finally she was finished. She brought Night Owl out, tied him to the cross-tie outside his stall and started to groom him. She loved to be all alone in the barn. It reminded her of early mornings at Windcroft when she would go out and feed the horses. Kate paused in her work and leaned against Night Owl, thinking of home. Her mother or Jessie would be in the barn right now, filling up the hay racks and replenishing the water buckets. Homesickness nibbled at her, but she ignored it. She was determined to make this time at Langwald work out well. But how? He kept giving her such a rough time. Even Casey had noticed it. Sure, everyone got ordered around, but it was like he never saw anything good in her. Kate kept trying and trying. She couldn't just give up. But some days she felt like it. Whenever she got really down, though, she would think about the camp horse-trials coming up in two weeks. Langwald wasn't judging them, and he wouldn't be in the middle of the ring yelling at her, either. She'd show him then. She was going for the blue ribbon.

She swung her saddle up onto Night Owl, put on his bridle and led him out into the clear summer day. It was going to be a hot one, but right now the early morning temperature was perfect. Kate walked Night Owl slowly around the ring savoring it all, finally feeling relaxed. When the horse was awake and ready to work, Kate put him through his paces, then over a couple of low fences. He felt supple and responsive beneath her.

"Hey, you're looking good." It was Trevor, leaning against the fence.

"Thanks," Kate said, and smiled. She headed Night Owl into a three-foot brush jump. He sailed over it.

"He looks like he's bored with those little jumps," called Trevor.

"You think so?" said Kate.

"Yeah, give him something to contend with," Trevor said. "Like the stone wall."

Kate trotted Night Owl in a small circle, signaled him into a canter, then pointed him at the middle of the stone wall. It was solid and ominous looking, but Kate could feel that Night Owl was under control. The horse adjusted his pace and took off at exactly the right spot. Up, up he climbed until the jump below looked like a faraway cliff to Kate. And then he came down, flexing as he hit the ground for a smooth landing. Kate wanted to shout with joy. It was a perfect jump. She looked to Trevor enthusiastically, and saw him grinning broadly.

"That was a beauty," he said. "A real beauty. Do you mind if I join you? I mean, have you had enough time to work out alone."

"Yeah, I'm fine now," said Kate. She watched Trevor walk toward the barn. Dara was right. It was fun having a boyfriend who was into horses. Not that Trevor was a *boyfriend*, but a boy friend. Kate headed Night Owl to the stone wall again, not wanting to think about the subtle distinction any longer.

Soon after Trevor joined her, the others began filtering into the ring. Casey led Caroline's horse out, all groomed and tacked up, and tied him to the hitching post. Caroline sauntered over from the house and coolly mounted. Kate shook her head. No wonder Caroline and the Robber Baron never looked connected. They didn't know each other. It was only their superb skill that got them through the courses in decent form, but they would never be champions. At the top level of competition, the subtleties count for more and more. You can't develop that extra dimension of communication if you and your horse don't know each other inside out.

"Okay, class," said Langwald, striding into the ring. He was his usual impeccable self, but he looked pale and very tired to Kate. "I presume you're all sufficiently warmed up."

Kate looked anxiously around for Dara, but she was nowhere in sight. Kate kicked herself for not going back up after breakfast to make sure Dara had gotten out of bed. Langwald was going to chew her out if she didn't get here soon. Like now.

"What we're going to work on this morning is the extension you must demand from your horses in order for them to perform at the upper levels of competition. You will begin to meet bigger and bigger oxers, jumps two and three poles wide."

Kate wiggled excitedly in her saddle, forgetting about Dara for a moment. Night Owl wouldn't have any problem with that. He had always loved to jump.

"You'll see that I've set up some new jumps in here," continued Langwald. "You'll go one at a time and start with the brush, then the double oxer, the gate, come around over the curved wall, and end with the triple oxer."

Kate couldn't wait to put Night Owl into those jumps. He was going to love it. She scanned the grounds once more for Dara, feeling anxious for her friend. Please, oh please, get up, Dara, she prayed.

"You'll go in your usual order," said Langwald. "Mr. Williams, you're up first, Miss O'Connell on deck. Everyone else out of the way."

Kate loved to watch Trevor and Paint-Patch work. They made such a smooth team. Nothing very spectacular, but the ultimate in communication between horse and rider. You could just see them adjusting for each other; helping each other out.

Kate hadn't seen Casey jump in a while and was surprised at how much she had improved. Something was different, really different. Kate stared hard but couldn't put her finger on it. Casey was draped in some big, floppy T-shirt as always. Maybe she'd lengthened her stirrups or shortened her reins a tad. Maybe, but it was hard to tell. The whole picture of Casey on Sweetpea was just much better.

And then it was Kate's turn. She circled Night Owl slowly, then pointed him at the first jump at a full canter. Up and over, up and over, one jump after the other. Kate reined in, grinning broadly.

"You've got to get more extension out of that horse, if you ever plan to compete in the upper levels," said Langwald.

Kate felt her face drop down around her knees. They'd had a perfect round, hadn't even ticked a jump. Okay, the jumps weren't very high, maybe two feet, nine inches, but why couldn't Langwald say something good about their performance?

"Get to the back of the line and do it again," ordered Langwald. "Try to keep your weight a bit more forward on those oxers. More pressure with the legs. It might help him extend."

Kate rode down the line of riders, feeling embarrassed. She caught Trevor's eye. "I thought you were great," he whispered as she rode by. Kate smiled at him.

Kate's second round was almost faultless, although Night Owl ticked the last pole of the last oxer.

"These are not big jumps, class," said Langwald, but Kate knew he was talking directly to her. "You'll be meeting much bigger ones in the trials. Those horses have got to really stretch. You've got to make them."

Kate turned at the sound of the gate behind her. Dara rode in. Everyone seemed to hold their breath, waiting for Langwald to attack. Kate's heart was beating so hard it ached. Dara smiled weakly at her. Poor Dara, thought Kate. Is she ever going to catch it now.

"Miss Cooper," said Langwald. "If you're ready, I'd like you to take your horse over the brush, the double oxer, the gate, curved wall, and finally the triple oxer."

Dara nodded coolly, circled, signaled Arpeggio into a canter at just the right minute, and sailed over the course.

"Now that's extension," said Langwald, when Dara reined in. "Did you see how that horse almost separated himself in the middle to make those jumps look effortless. Very good, Miss Cooper." He took a deep breath and continued. "I would like you to polish all the brass doorknobs and hinges on the stable doors this afternoon to remind you how much it displeases me when my students can't give me the respect of arriving for class on time. Do I make myself clear?"

"Yes sir," said Dara, obviously relieved there wasn't going to be more of a scene.

Kate stared at Langwald with her mouth hanging open. If I'd shown up late for class he would have fried me for dinner, she thought angrily. But no, Dara can show up any old time and he goes on and on about what a great rider she is. Well, I'm a great rider, too. Why, why, why can't he see that? Why does he see me as such a failure?

Chapter 7

"I know what," Kate said, taking the can that plopped down from the drink machine. "Let's rearrange the whole barn. I mean, just as a joke. It'll still be neat, everything will just be in a new place. We could even put the horses in different stalls and change the name plates all around." Kate laughed at the whole idea. "Fangwald would go nuts."

"Why do you keep fighting him?" asked Dara as she propped her feet up on the coffee table in the rec room. Dinner was over and, for once, Langwald didn't have an after-dinner training movie or lecture for them. It felt good just to relax. Other kids were wandering around, reading magazines, watching TV or talking in small groups.

"Casey, can I get you a soda while I'm up?" Kate asked, purposely ignoring Dara's remark.

"No ... no thanks."

"A candy bar? They've got those chocolate things you like."

"Thanks anyway, but no."

"What's this?" Dara asked, sitting up. "Casey O'Connell refusing food?"

"I'm trying to learn a little discipline," said Casey.

"Uh-oh," broke in Kate. "The Langwald System has finally gotten to poor old Casey."

"Maybe it's not such a bad system," said Dara. "Have you ever thought about that?"

"Maybe it's not," snapped Kate. "But it certainly isn't working for me."

"How do you know?" Dara asked.

"All he does is yell at me ... constantly," replied Kate.

"I've never heard him yell," said Dara. "Have you, Casey?"

"Nope. Rant and rave—yes, but yell—no," Casey said.

"See," said Kate.

"Not really. Maybe he's trying to tell you something that you're just not hearing," Dara insisted.

"Yeah, like I'm the worst rider he's ever had at his camp," Kate said. She twirled her can nervously in her hands.

"I think you should listen a little closer," said Dara. She exchanged looks with Casey.

"It's easy for you to say all this." Kate was on the verge of sulking. "He adores you. He didn't even give you a rough time that morning you overslept."

"No, but he made me polish brass until all my dreams were in shades of gold. And I must admit, I haven't been late for a class since," said Dara.

"It's not the same," Kate said.

"Of course it's not," said Casey. "You're different people. He deals with you in different ways."

"Well, I wish he'd get off my back."

"No one move," whispered Casey. "The best thing since banana splits just walked in and he's headed this way!"

"Good evening, ladies," said Trevor, bowing gallantly.

Kate shifted uncertainly in her chair, Casey turned bright red and Dara smiled warmly.

"The moon should be full tonight," Trevor said, turning to Kate. "I was wondering if you'd like to go for that ride we talked about?"

"Uh-Uh . . ." stammered Kate.

"About ten," said Trevor.

"That's after lights out," blurted out Casey.

"I'll go," said Kate suddenly. How wonderful to break a few rules around this boot camp. "I'd love to."

Trevor smiled broadly. "Great. Meet you in the barn just before ten."

Kate felt a surge of confidence. Might as well have some fun. She grinned at Dara and Casey.

"Some people have all the luck," Casey said as she watched Trevor walk out of the room. "I'd give anything to have that hunk as my boyfriend."

"He's not my boyfriend," insisted Kate.

"You're going out for a friendly moonlight ride?" teased Dara.

"Ah yes," joined in Casey. "There's talk of a nighttime cross-country course being added to the next Olympics and you want to get a jump on training."

"Get a *jump* on training," laughed Dara. "Good one, O'Connell."

They all laughed.

"Well," said Kate through her giggles. "Laughing at that stupid joke just proves we're all finally cracking up."

"This is true," said Casey with mock solemnity. "This is indeed true."

They started laughing all over again.

"Okay," said Dara. "Before we get any worse, I'm going to wash my hair and then write a few letters."

"Now, I wonder who you're writing to?" teased Kate. "Doug, Douglas, and Dougie, I bet."

"Ah, you're just jealous," said Dara with a grin.

"*Moi*," said Kate. "*Moi*, who is going out with the ... how did Casey put it ... the best thing since banana splits?"

Dara giggled.

"I wish I could disguise myself as you and take your place," moaned Casey.

"I wish you could, too," said Kate, "but I wouldn't give up breaking one of Fangwald's rules for anything in the world."

"I couldn't go anyway, I've got three pairs of Caroline's boots to polish by tomorrow morning." Casey made a face.

"I don't know why you cater to that Southern belle," said Dara.

"Yeah, it would do her riding a world of good if she did some work herself," Kate added.

"Well, I want to buy a new jacket for the horse show ... in size 5," said Casey with determination. "So I need the work."

"What do you think, Elsinore of Bodiam," Kate

said as she stood in front of her favorite picture in her bedroom. "Is this Trevor Williams the white knight of my dreams as everyone says?"

"Are you talking to that picture again?" asked Dara. She was curled up on the bed with her hair wrapped in a towel, scribbling away.

"Yes." Kate pulled a comb through her long blond hair and continued. "It's the one thing around this place that doesn't argue with me."

Dara laughed. "It is a beautiful horse," she said. "I wonder who it was or is. Is there a date on the picture?"

"No," said Kate. "There's only the name—Elsinore of Bodiam. Isn't that romantic?"

"Don't get too romantic," said Dara. "Remember you're going on this moonlight ride just to get back at Langwald."

"Fangwald."

"Right."

The air was cool after the hot day. Kate breathed in deeply, as much to calm herself as to enjoy the sweet smells of a country night. The barns and fields were bathed in a pale silver moonlight, horses were silhouetted on the crests of hills, crickets and tree frogs sang out to their hearts' content. Kate noticed a light in the private barn behind the house, so she kept to the shadows as she made her way to the stables. She slipped in the side door through the tack room to avoid the noise the big doors would make. It was dark inside, but she knew just where her bridle hung. She worried for a moment when she remembered that Langwald made a tack check at the end of

each day. She shook her nervousness away and
plucked the bridle off its hook and entered the
main section of the barn.

"Kate?" The whisper seemed to leap out of the
dark.

"Yes ... Trevor?"

A few horses shifted their weight at the sound
of the voices. Night Owl rumbled a low greeting
as if he understood the need for quiet.

Trevor approached her in the dark and put a
hand on her shoulder. He was warm and had a
different smell than the barn—all soapy and
clean. She could see the white of his teeth when
he smiled.

"I'm so glad you came," he said. "Let's go."

"I didn't get my saddle," whispered Kate.

"That's fine," Trevor replied. "Bareback is less
fuss."

"Less fuss, less noise," Kate said. "I saw a light
in the barn behind the house."

"Me, too. I think it must be Langwald. Dr. Andrews' van is in the driveway, too. They sure
spend a lot of time out there."

"Doing what?"

"I have no idea. Probably plotting new exercises to torture us with."

Kate giggled.

"We'll take the horses out the back door, away
from the house," Trevor said.

"Okay. See you there in a minute."

Night Owl's stall opened noiselessly when Kate
entered and for once she was glad that she'd
oiled the hinges. She laughed to herself at the
irony of it—Langwald would flip out if he knew

his careful orders were actually helping her break his rules.

Night Owl nudged her affectionately when she got near. Kate gave him a carrot, then slipped the bridle on and led him outside. Trevor was already there. They mounted without speaking and moved away from the farm at a walk. Slowly they wound up the hill at the back. Kate felt as though she were moving in a dream. It was all so unreal—the light, the amplified sound of the horses' hooves on the path, the silky feeling of the night air.

They rode for twenty minutes, Trevor in the lead. Finally at the top of the hill he reined in, and waited for her to catch up.

"Isn't this amazing?" he said in a hushed voice.

"Unbelievable," whispered Kate. The magical full moon seemed almost within reach. It splashed the sky above and the land below with a fragile silver wash. Trees stood out in dark relief against the pale hills. The river was a filament of twisted silver inlaid in the valley floor, the farm a fairy lair nestled at the foot of the hill. The one light in the barn still shone brightly like beacon.

Trevor slipped off his horse, then holding Night Owl's bridle, helped Kate dismount. They tied the horses to a tree and sat down to savor the scene. The ground beneath them still held the day's warmth. The grass had a pungent, sweet smell. Kate sighed deeply.

"This is so wonderfully peaceful," she said. "Even I don't feel like fighting anything."

Trevor laughed, deep and low in his chest. "You do try to wrestle the world to the ground at least once a day, don't you?"

"I'm not that bad." Kate laughed.

"I didn't say it was bad," Trevor noted, then added, "I admire you for it. I wish I had more of your fighting spirit. I'd be a better rider for it, that's for sure."

Kate basked in the praise. It was nice to have someone who approved of her. Her ego had taken such a bashing from Langwald and now it seemed that even Dara and Casey were agreeing with him. Kate sighed deeply again, then felt all her muscles tighten when Trevor put his arm around her. She tried to will herself to relax again, but she couldn't.

"I like you, Kate," said Trevor, tightening his hold on her.

"I like you, too," she replied, not knowing exactly what to say. She had the feeling that the conversation and the evening were getting out of her control, and she couldn't decide if this was a good feeling or a bad one.

"I was hoping you did," said Trevor. They lapsed into silence again. Kate concentrated hard on the landscape before them, hoping Trevor couldn't feel her heart beating itself to pieces.

"I'll really miss you when camp ends," said Trevor eventually.

Kate looked up into his face. It, too, was bathed in magic, silver light. He looked more handsome than ever. Kate swallowed hard. "Yeah, we've had some fun times together," she said, trying to keep things light. Then she felt his skin against hers. She tasted his lips. Her stomach flip-flopped and her skin felt like it was jumping all over the place. But one image dominated her mind. Pete! Pete smiling at her with his crooked grin. Kate pulled back.

"I . . . I can't, Trevor."

"Oh Kate, I really care for you," he pleaded.

"Th-that's not it," stammered Kate, unsure herself of what she was feeling.

"But I thought you liked me."

"I do. I do," insisted Kate. "But . . ."

"And we get along so well," said Trevor, holding her hand tenderly in his. "You laugh at my stupid jokes, I laugh at yours."

"Yeah, you've really helped me keep it together around this place," said Kate.

"Right," Trevor agreed. "We're partners."

"We're friends," Kate said.

"Just friends?"

"Yes."

"That guy you mentioned?"

"I think so."

Trevor was quiet for a moment, staring out over the valley, his profile in silhouette to Kate. She felt intensely sad. Looking at his face, she realized how important Trevor really had become to her and now she was turning him away. And for what? Pete? They hadn't spoken to each other in almost a month. She had no idea where he was or what he was thinking. And here was this warm, wonderful person who could share her world as Pete never could. Maybe I really am going nuts, thought Kate, shaking her head. Trevor squeezed her hand.

"Then that's one lucky guy," he said quietly. "I hope he realizes it."

A tear slid down Kate's cheek. I just hope he

knows I'm alive, she thought, then said aloud, "Well, I think I'm pretty lucky to know you."

"Yeah ... maybe," said Trevor sadly. He pulled Kate to her feet. "We better head back. The light in the barn went off about ten minutes ago."

Kate opened her bedroom door without making a sound and got ready for bed in the dark. Her heart was heavy. Trevor hadn't said a word the whole way back. She couldn't bear the thought that she'd lost his friendship, but what could she do? She had thought maybe they could be more to each other than just friends. But she couldn't. It just didn't feel right.

Kate fumbled in her suitcase and found her writing paper, grabbed Dara's flashlight from her night table where she always kept it and got into bed and under the covers.

"Wiley, just what are you doing?" came Dara's sleepy voice a few minutes later.

"I'm writing a letter."

"At this time of night!" Kate heard Dara scrounging around for her watch. "It's eleven-thirty! Who rates that?"

"Pete."

Chapter 8

TREVOR had avoided her all week. When they had met at meals or during classes in the ring, he had been pleasant, but his smile had lost its sparkle. And, no longer did he hang on the fence when she worked out in the ring, offering pointers, no longer were the chores fun; they got drearier and drearier without Trevor's humor. No longer did the sad face of the moon make her smile. Kate felt lost without his friendship.

"Why don't you just sit down and talk it out with him?" suggested Dara, as she tightened Arpeggio's girth. Her face was tanned from being outdoors day after day, and her hair was streaked with pale yellow from the sun.

She's thriving on this place, thought Kate, looking at her friend. She actually likes it. Then aloud she said, "I've tried. He says he's just not ready." Kate swung her saddle up on Night Owl. It landed too hard and Night Owl's ears shot back. He flicked his tail anxiously back and forth.

"Give him time then," said Dara.

"There isn't much time," Kate said. "The trials are in a week and then it's bye-bye Langwald's."

"I'm actually going to miss this place," said Dara, glancing around.

"Well, I'm not." Kate eased the bit into Night Owl's mouth and pulled the top of the bridle over his ears.

"Come on," prodded Dara. "Admit it. Your riding has really improved since you've been here."

"Tell that to Fangwald."

"Forget him for a minute. How do you feel about the training you've gotten?"

"Let's just say it would be hard to eat, sleep and breathe horses for a month without improving," Kate said.

The girls led their horses out of the barn and mounted up. "Well, I think we've improved an awful lot," said Dara.

"The trials will tell us that," Kate said. "I want to do really well. Just to prove to Langwald he's got me all wrong."

"Maybe you've got him all wrong," suggested Dara.

"There you go again, making me look like the villain."

"I'm sorry, Kate," Dara said. "I just want you to be happy."

The girls walked their horses along in silence toward the outside course. Langwald was going to devote the whole morning to pacing the course.

"No, I'm sorry," said Kate. "I've been acting like a real pill. I don't know what's wrong with me. Maybe I'm just uptight about the trials. I absolutely must do well, or I might as well give up."

"You're going to do great," said Dara. "You are a fabulous rider, believe me."

"I'd like to."

"Race you to the river," Dara challenged. She urged Arpeggio forward.

Immediately Kate gave Night Owl his lead. The horses galloped neck and neck for the first hundred yards, then Night Owl pulled ahead just before the drop to the river. The girls reined in on the bank, laughing.

"Maybe Night Owl should be a racehorse," giggled Kate. "Give up this combined training stuff."

"Maybe so," said Dara solemnly.

"Hey, I was only kidding," said Kate, whirling Night Owl around. "Race you back!"

The two horses finished neck and neck. Night Owl pranced around excitedly when they stopped, eager for more play. Kate patted his neck to calm him down.

"Easy, Bird. Time to get serious. Here comes the Big Hoof."

Dara laughed. They watched Langwald march across the fields toward them. The other riders were gathering at the start of the outside course.

"I wonder why we've never seen Langwald on horseback," whispered Dara.

"I don't know," Kate replied. "Maybe he can't ride."

The girls managed to smother their giggles just as Langwald reached the group.

"Good morning, class," he said. "As you know, this morning we're going to concentrate on pacing—that is, knowing just how hard to push your horse around this tough course. I'm certain most of your horses can actually get over these various jumps; but can you maintain a constant, accelerated pace? This is the real challenge and where you can lose a lot of points in competition. Okay, we'll go in the usual order."

Kate and Night Owl eyed the cross-country course eagerly. This was their favorite event of the three that made up the combined training regimen—dressage, cross country, and stadium jumping. And Langwald's had a particularly beautiful course, the jumps following the natural roll of the land. From each rise was an intimate view into another section of the valley, not that you had time to ponder it when you were flying over three-foot obstacles. Kate could feel that Night Owl was raring to go, but they had to watch the others go first.

"That looked great," Kate whispered to Trevor after he finished his round.

He looked at her distractedly. "Thanks," he said, then moved away to the other side of the group.

Caroline was up and everyone watched as she headed over the jumps. Kate held her breath. Horse and rider just weren't in sync. She could tell that Caroline was giving signals that interrupted the horse's natural rhythm. He got over the jumps but he was always jumping too early or too late. Suddenly, at the water jump, Caroline pulled back on the reins just as the Robber Baron took off. His balance was thrown totally off and he crashed into the planks before the water. Everyone gasped in horror as Caroline flew over the horse's head.

"Roll!" yelled Langwald. "Keep rolling, Caroline!"

Caroline hit the ground and rolled over and over to get out of the way of the Baron's hoofs and his body if he fell. He floundered in the water for a few moments, then found his footing and waded out. Langwald ran over to Caroline, but she was already on her feet. She grabbed the Baron's reins and, without a word, stomped off toward the barn. Kate was surprised by this reaction from Caroline. She had stayed outside the group from the first day, walking around as if Langwald's and everyone there bored her to death.

"All right, class," said Langwald. "I think you can see the importance of pacing over these jumps. Let the horse tell you what to do. Feel it and go with him. Okay, Miss Wiley, you're up."

Kate shifted her weight forward and pressed the Owl's sides with her legs. Night Owl knew the signal and broke immediately into a trot. More pressure from Kate and he switched smoothly into a canter. Kate urged him into the fastest pace she felt he could handle on this course and Night Owl responded. The first jump flowed by and the next and the next. Kate could feel the lay of the land beneath them as Night Owl flexed and moved over it. They were connected. Then, at the next jump, a post and rails, Night Owl suddenly pulled out at the last minute. Kate was thrown to one side and just barely managed to stay on.

"Night Owl!" she whispered harshly, circling him back around. "What are you doing? Get yourself over this jump."

She headed him into it again and again he pulled out.

"Hit him with your crop!" shouted Langwald. "He's playing games with you."

Kate glared at Langwald. She carried a crop during training, but she'd never used it. She couldn't imagine striking Night Owl.

"Bird, get your buns over this jump," she said, and squeezed him into action with her legs. This time he slid to a halt right in front of the jump and again Kate was almost unseated. By the time she got Night Owl back in position for another try, Langwald was beside her.

"If this were a trial, Wiley, one more refusal and you'd be disqualified. How does that make you feel?"

"I don't know what's wrong with him," said Kate, close to tears. She couldn't believe Night Owl would let her down on the outside course.

"Well, I do," barked Langwald. "He's not in the mood. These piddling little planks aren't challenging enough for him, so he's not going to do it. Get off him."

Kate didn't know what Langwald had in mind, but she dismounted. He took the reins from her and mounted Night Owl with a practiced ease. Kate watched in horror as he pulled his riding crop from his boot and whacked Night Owl soundly on the rump. Night Owl's ears shot forward and he pranced energetically. Langwald circled him, whacked him again, and took him over the jump. He made it with a foot to spare.

"There," said Langwald, handing Night Owl back to Kate. "I think he understands who's in control now."

Speechless with anger, Kate took Night Owl from Langwald and stormed back to the group. Never, never had Night Owl been treated so roughly. It was unthinkable to beat him. She patted his neck comfortingly as she rejoined the group.

"Horses used for eventing, class, are not pets," said Langwald. "They are highly trained machines. Consistency is what you're looking for in them."

You're a highly trained machine, Kate raged inside. You wouldn't know a feeling or emotion if you tripped over it.

"Okay," continued Langwald. "Class dismissed. Reconvene back here at one o'clock. I think you could all use some extra work."

"Kate, wait up!" called Dara, running after Kate as she stomped back to the house. "I thought you were supposed to sweep out the barn. Where are you going in such a rush?"

"Home."

"Home? What are you talking about?"

"I'm bailing out. I've had it with this place. Langwald hitting Night Owl was the last straw. The last straw, I tell you."

"He got Night Owl over the jump, didn't he?"

"Sure, I guess you can beat anyone into anything."

"But, Kate," pleaded Dara, grabbing Kate's arm. "Maybe he was right. Night Owl was losing interest in the course. I could see that from where I was. He loves those big, nasty jumps, but he was getting sloppy over the easier ones."

"He didn't have to beat him," said Kate, yanking back her arm and striding away from Dara. She paused in the hallway of the house to see if any mail had come for her. It hadn't. Her spirits plummeted further. Pete was bound to have her letter by now. Why didn't he write or call or something. Kate dragged herself upstairs, pulled out her suitcase and began throwing in her clothes. Suddenly it occurred to her that there was no way her parents could pick her and Night Owl up with one day's notice. She was stuck here for at least another day. Best to go call and get things moving from the other end, though.

Dara was sitting on the porch steps waiting for her when she came out. "Now where are you going?" she asked, jumping to her feet.

"To use the pay phone in the barn. I've got to get Mother to organize the van to come get me."

"I'll go with you," said Dara, trotting along beside her.

Kate listened to the phone in her home ring and ring, each unanswered ring stinging like another rejection.

"They're probably all at the barn," Dara suggested.

"Oh ... right," said Kate. She dialed the other number. "I'm not thinking very clearly."

"Hello!"

Kate almost burst into tears when Jessie answered. "Jess, it's me! Kate!" She turned to Dara. "It's Jessie, Dara! It's Jessie!"

"Great. Talk to her."

"Right." Kate turned back to the receiver. "Jess, I'm coming home."

"Why?" asked Jessie in surprise. "Did you get hurt? Is Night Owl okay?"

"Yeah, I'm just sick of this place. It's like a marine camp, and this morning Langwald hit Night Owl to get him over a jump."

"Did he deserve it?"

"Who?"

"Well, dummy, I certainly didn't mean Langwald." Jessie laughed.

Kate laughed, too. "Of course he didn't. You know I never beat Night Owl."

"Well, I can recall a couple of times it might have done him good," said Jessie. "But, let's not get into that. I'm just telling you you can't come home."

"Why?" asked Kate in confusion.

"Because then I'd have to cancel my plans to come visit."

"You're coming up? Really!" shouted Kate excitedly. "Dara, Jessie's coming up!"

"When? When?" both girls cried into the mouthpiece at once.

"Well, I thought I'd come up for the trials next weekend, but it sounds like you could use a little moral support right now," said Jessie. "I'll get up as soon as I can."

"Yahooo!" exclaimed Kate.

"Oh Kate, hang on, your mom's just coming in from riding," said Jessie. "I'll put her on."

"Katie May!" said Anne Wiley into the phone. "It is really you?"

Kate could hardly answer, the tears were choking her so. "Yes, Mom, how are you? How's the old leg?"

"I'm back in action," said Anne proudly. "I've schooled Northern Spy every day this week and the leg feels stronger and stronger."

"Mom, that's wonderful!" cried Kate. "Any takers for Spy yet?"

"Well ... no," said Anne. "Of course, with me

being on crutches, I couldn't really keep him in shape. But Pietro called last night and he's getting very anxious to find Spy a good home, so I guess I have to start taking it more seriously. Put out some advertisements, things like that."

"He's a magnificent horse, moves like a dream," Kate said. "I'm sure you won't have any trouble selling him."

"No, it's just that Pietro isn't interested in the highest bidder, he wants just the right person," said Anne. "You know how he is about that horse. I think Spy is the son he never had."

"Yeah, I think you're right," Kate agreed.

Before Kate knew it, she'd been on the phone forty minutes going back and forth between Jessie and her mother, catching up on all the news from the farm. Finally she said good-bye and hung up.

"Uh ... you forgot to tell your mother to send the van for you," said Dara mischievously.

"Oh my gosh!" said Kate. "You're right. But ... I don't have any more change."

"Guess you can't call back then, huh?"

"Guess not," replied Kate, then jumped into the air. "Jessie's coming!"

Dara went up with her on the next jump. "Yahoo!" they both howled.

Chapter 9

"HEY ... Dara ... over here!" yelled Kate, waving her paintbrush. "I saved you a brush."

Dara caught sight of Kate in the tangle of jumps and people. Everyone was in the ring getting it in shape for next week's trials. Some were stuffing cedar boughs into jumps, some painting, some measuring to get the distances between the jumps just right. The excitement and high spirits vibrated in the air.

"I'm not in the mood for this," groaned Dara, taking the offered paintbrush and dipping it into the bucket of green paint.

"Where've you been anyway?" asked Kate.

"Guess?"

"Well, by the look on your face, I'd say you've been on the phone with Doug," Kate said. She propped up another pole and began painting the white stripes, leaving the green ones for Dara.

"Bingo," said Dara.

81

"And ... it didn't go so hot," continued Kate.

"Remember that dance at the club I told you about?" said Dara.

"The big midsummer ball?"

"Yeah. He just reminded me it's this coming weekend."

"You forgot?"

Dara turned to Kate. "I've been living and breathing horses for the past month," she said with annoyance. "Of course I forgot."

"What are you going to do?" asked Kate.

"There's nothing I can do. We've got the trials this weekend." Dara slapped angrily at the pole with her brush, splattering paint. "And horses come before boys. Remember?"

"I take it Doug had a hard time understanding that."

"As usual," Dara said. She splashed on more paint. "I tell you I have a hard time understanding it, too, sometimes. Maybe I ought to give him up ... or maybe just give up horses."

"Dara! How can you say something like that?" exclaimed Kate. "Of course you can't give up horses! I mean, can you actually imagine life without Arpeggio?"

"Well, I don't think I can give up Doug," said Dara mournfully. "I really care for him. I just wish he'd understand my commitment to riding and combined training."

"Yeah," said Kate. "Makes me realize how wonderful Pete always was about my time with Night Owl."

"Have you heard from him yet?" asked Dara.

"Nope," Kate replied, feeling a jab of pain in

her heart. "Don't worry. You'll be the first to know."

"Gosh, I'm really sorry," said Dara, then added quickly, "Maybe he didn't get the letter."

"Yeah ... maybe," Kate said, concentrating even harder on her painting. She found herself thinking more and more about Pete these days. She'd be going home in a week. But to what? For all she knew he might be seeing someone else. Why else hadn't he gotten in touch with her in almost a month?

"What about Trevor?" asked Dara. "Is that over as in *over*?"

"There was nothing to be over, I keep telling you," said Kate. "We are ... were ... friends. That's it."

"You mean you never thought there could ever be anything?"

Kate hesitated, remembering her attraction to Trevor at first. But that was the kind of guy he was. Everyone loved Trevor. Like everyone loved Pete. A light suddenly went on in Kate's head.

"You know," she said thoughtfully, "I think I was attracted to the Peteness in Trevor."

"The what?" exclaimed Dara, pausing in her work. Green paint dribbled from her brush all over her sneakers.

"The *Peteness*. That's it, Dara! Don't you see?" said Kate excitedly.

"Actually ... no," said Dara, the paint still dripping away.

"Well ... okay ... I admit it, I was attracted to Trevor for a while and that was really confusing, 'cause I thought it was only Pete who could make me feel all mushy and crazy and stuff."

"I know the feeling," Dara sighed.

"But what was really attracting me was a few of the qualities Trevor has that are like Pete's." Kate started pacing back and forth, gesturing with her paintbrush. "You know, they're both really friendly, not tripping over their fat egos all the time. They have a way of making everyone happy. That stuff."

"Yeah, I can see that," said Dara, suddenly noticing the dripping paint and yanking her foot out of the way.

"I kept trying to force things in my head with Trevor," continued Kate. "It just never felt right, though."

"And it still doesn't?" asked Dara.

"I don't think so," said Kate. "I miss him, though. You know, just kidding around with him. He was a good friend."

"Boys are more work than Langwald's." Dara sighed and turning back to her painting.

"Yeah," agreed Kate. The girls worked side by side in silence. Finally Kate said, "Do you think Jessie will make it up today?"

"I hope so. I told Langwald she was coming and he said he'd have an extra cot put in our room."

Kate looked at Dara with surprise. "Gosh, he almost sounds human."

"He is, Kate," said Dara. "You just won't give him a chance."

"He won't give me a chance is more like it," Kate said.

Both girls looked up at the sound of a car coming up the drive.

"It's just Dr. Andrews," announced Kate with

disappointment. "I wonder what he's doing here all the time."

They watched the old vet's van pull up in front of the house. Dr. Andrews got out and walked quickly back to the private barn behind the house. Kate and Dara looked at each other.

"I wonder what goes on back there," said Kate.

"Probably just a sick horse," said Dara. "Langwald has enough horses around here to keep a vet pretty busy."

"Not that busy," said Kate. "Dr. Andrews is here at least every other day."

"Yeah, it does seem a little weird," Dara said.

"Look at Caroline," said Kate with a giggle.

Caroline was painting the brick pattern on a wall jump very gingerly.

"Has she been working on that all afternoon?" asked Dara.

"Well, ever since Langwald made her come out," said Kate. "She tried to plead sick to get out of work but he didn't buy it."

"Let's go help her," suggested Dara. "She'll never get finished and everyone else is winding things up."

The girls walked over to Caroline and offered their services.

"No, I can manage," said Caroline, not even bothering to look up at them. "I work better alone."

Dara and Kate looked at each other and rolled their eyes.

"How about we take the horses for a swim," Casey shouted across the ring. Her big T-shirt was splattered with red paint.

"All right!" everyone agreed. They slapped lids

on paint cans, cleaned up the brushes and rushed to get their horses. In five minutes flat, the ring was deserted except for Caroline. Everyone else was in the stables putting bridles on their horses. Then there was a mad rush to the river. The cool water felt good on their hot, tired bodies. And even the horses seemed to be enjoying it, pawing at the water with their hooves, dipping their noses in, then throwing their heads back, spraying water everywhere.

When Kate saw Trevor in front of her, she couldn't resist. She kicked a huge arc of water at him. It splashed his back and ran off Paint-Patch in waterfalls.

"Hey!" he cried and whirled Paint around. They charged Kate and Night Owl. Laughing, Kate wheeled Night Owl out of the way but not before Trevor managed to drench them both. Kate kicked back. Then Trevor. Others joined in and the water churned wildly as they all splashed. Finally Kate headed Night Owl out into the middle of the river. It was deep and soon she could feel him lose contact with the bottom and begin to swim. Trevor and Paint swam up beside them. The horses swam to the other side and clambered up the bank. Kate and Trevor reined them in side by side and watched the others cavort. Finally the horses caught their breath and a peaceful quiet settled over them.

"Are you looking forward to the trials?" Trevor asked.

"Yeah," said Kate. "Are you?"

"I think so. It will be interesting to see just how much I have improved here."

Kate glanced over at him. His gentle blue eyes reflected the sky and his wet hair clinging in spiky curls to his forehead and temples made him look somehow vulnerable.

"Kate ... I ..." he began haltingly, not daring to look at her. His forlorn voice made Kate's heart ache, but before he could continue, they were interrupted.

"Kate! Kate!"

Kate whirled around. Across the river Dara was waving both her arms wildly from atop Arpeggio.

"Jessie's here! Look!" Dara pointed toward the farm. Jessie was standing on top of the fence, searching the gaggle of horses and riders. Kate waved. Jessie saw her and waved back.

"Come on, Kate," yelled Dara, turning Arpeggio toward the farm. "She's here! She's here!"

Kate turned her excited face back to Trevor. "My friend Jessie's arrived!" she bubbled.

He smiled warmly at her. "Go," he said.

"But you wanted to say something," said Kate.

"It can wait," said Trevor.

Kate searched his face one last time, then spurred Night Owl toward Jessie.

Chapter 10

"OKAY, Jess, I want you to tell me what you really think," said Kate, setting Night Owl up for the first jump in the ring.

Jessie readjusted her position on the fence. "Okay, but I'm so tired I can hardly keep my eyes open. When did we finally get to sleep last night?"

"I don't know. About two, I think," said Kate.

"Ohhh," groaned Jessie. "No wonder I'm about to fall over. You and Dara forced me to tell you absolutely everything that's happened at Windcroft every minute of every day since you've been gone. I'm exhausted."

"Yeah ... sorry," said Kate sheepishly. "We've just been a little homesick up here."

"I'll say," Jessie said. "Now show me this new, improved riding ability."

"Well, it's not new and I certainly don't know how improved it is," admitted Kate. "I told you about Langwald."

"Yeah, he sounds like a real bear," said Jessie. "I'm not sure I ever want to meet him."

"Forget about him right now," said Kate. "Just tell me how Night Owl looks going over these things."

"Okay, go ahead."

Kate took Night Owl over a series of jumps, then reined in in front of Jessie.

"Well?" she asked.

"Wow! I've never seen him jumping so good," said Jessie enthusiastically. "I mean it. You look great. And he's really getting his feet up. I didn't know he had it in him. I'm impressed."

"You make it sound like he used to be pretty lousy," said Kate defensively.

"You've got to admit, Night Owl has had good days and bad days," said Jessie.

"Haven't we all?" said Kate.

"Don't bite my head off," said Jessie. "I'm your friend, remember? Take it for what it's worth. Night Owl is doing great."

"Isn't he!" said Dara, coming up just then with Arpeggio.

"Yeah, I was just telling Kate, I've never seen him jumping so well," said Jessie.

"I think they've both improved so much here," added Dara.

Kate looked from one to the other. Why did she get the feeling they were holding back something from her? She whirled Night Owl around and took him over another group of jumps. He sailed over the lot.

"It looks like that switching did him some good,"

said Langwald. Kate turned in surprise. She hadn't seen him come up to the side of the ring. "Wouldn't you agree?"

Kate felt torn. She hated to admit to Langwald that his mean behavior towards her horse might have actually done Night Owl some good, but she had to admit to herself that Night Owl was really paying attention to her today.

"I still don't think you have to hit a horse," said Kate defiantly.

"Some horses, no," said Langwald. He started to walk away, then turned back. "You're looking good, though."

"He seemed like a nice guy," said Jessie when Langwald had disappeared into the barn. "Who is he? One of your teachers?"

Kate's mouth had dropped in surprise. "That was Langwald!"

"But I thought you said he was so horrible." Jessie was confused. "I expected nothing less than horns and fangs."

"Didn't you hear what he said?" Kate asked, her voice rising. "He said Night Owl needed to have some sense beaten into him."

"He said *some* horses need it," Jessie said calmly. "And I suppose some horses do."

"Beating is a little harsh, I think," said Dara. "All Langwald did was swat Night Owl on the butt once or twice. He didn't draw blood."

Jessie giggled.

"I can't believe you two," said Kate. "I thought you were supposed to be my friends."

"We *are*, silly," said Jessie, glancing at Dara. "I

just think you've worked yourself up into a tizzy over Langwald."

"Yeah," Dara agreed. "He even said you were looking good and Langwald never compliments anyone."

"Humph," mumbled Kate. "Except you." She leaned over and patted Night Owl lovingly on his neck.

The ring and dressage arena was beginning to fill up with students getting in their last-minute practice before the trials. The air was filled with shouts of "heads up," as another horse and rider headed into a jump.

"I'm glad we got out here early," said Dara, riding Arpeggio out of the ring.

"Me, too," agreed Kate, following with Night Owl. "It's a zoo in there."

They rode up to where Jessie was sitting on the fence.

"Whew, you could cut the tension in that ring with a knife," she said.

"Yeah, everyone's a bit antsy about the trials," remarked Kate.

"Reminds me of my old stables back in Pennsylvania," Dara said, absentmindedly stroking Arpeggio's neck. "It got like this before every event. Best friends would be at each other's throats. Some friendships didn't even survive it. It was really horrible."

"I guess everyone wants to win," Kate said.

"I don't," said Jessie.

"Now, Jess, admit it," said Kate. "You love walking away with that old blue ribbon."

"Of course," agreed Jessie. "But I don't fall to pieces if I don't. I fall to pieces if I don't feel I've improved."

"Well, I can tell you," continued Kate, "everyone you see in that ring will be out for the blue on Saturday."

"How about you, Kate?" asked Dara.

"Sure."

For just a moment, there was a strained silence. Kate turned her concentration to Trevor, who was moving Paint-Patch very calmly in a routine through and around the other riders. Then the image of Pete wandered into her head. She tried to push it out, but it lingered.

"Well, Dara has to get at least one blue ribbon," Jessie teased, "to match the color of her new jacket. Or else, her mother will take her head off."

Dara laughed, Kate joined in and the tension melted.

"Since we've already worked out, what are we going to do with the rest of our morning?" Kate asked the other two, leading Night Owl into the barn.

"I told Langwald we'd take the horse trials posters to town and get them put up," said Dara. "Since Jessie has her Gran's car, I figured it wouldn't be a problem. Do you mind, Jess?"

"Not at all," Jessie replied. She helped Kate untack Night Owl. "You two can give me a tour of the area."

Kate and Dara glanced at each other and laughed. "This is the first time we've been off the farm," they said.

"You're kidding!" gasped Jessie.

"I wish we were," Dara said.

"Don't you get a day off?" asked Jessie.

"Sundays are free, but we're always so tired and we have to get our laundry done and no one has a car," Dara explained.

"My gosh, it's like boot camp or something," said Jessie, glancing around the organized barn.

"Now you're getting the picture," said Kate. She rubbed at the sweaty saddle mark on Night Owl's back with a damp sponge, then smoothed his hair back in place with the soft body-brush. He shifted his weight lazily over onto one side and whinnied softly.

"Do you wish you'd come up with us?" asked Dara.

Jessie looked around. "No. I mean ... I've missed you guys ... a lot. But I wouldn't have missed these days with Time Out and Tip-Toe for anything in the world. You know, Tip-Toe lets me pick up his feet and I even put a light saddle on him the other day," said Jessie enthusiastically. "I didn't do up the girth or anything like that. But he trusted me enough to take the saddle."

"That's wonderful, Jess," said Kate.

"Yeah, and you've had Amory to do things with," said Dara. "Sounds like you've had a pretty good summer so far."

"I have," agreed Jessie. "Of course, my actual riding has had to take second place, but even that's okay. I'll get back to it."

"We'll teach you all we've learned at Langwald's," teased Kate.

"You guys really have improved up here," said Jessie. "No kidding. I could tell just watching you this morning."

"You really think so?" asked Kate.

"Sure. You've left me way behind," said Jessie.

"Well, we'll have to see on Saturday," said Kate quietly.

"About your new coat, Dara. Is it all pressed and ready for the big event?" asked Jessie. "Your mother told me to remind you to wear it."

Dara rolled her eyes and sighed. "I'd hoped she'd forgotten."

"It's a beautiful jacket," Kate said. "Why don't you like it?"

"Because Mother picked it out," said Dara. "She didn't even ask me if I liked it and now I feel guilty that I don't want to wear it. It sits in my closet haunting me."

"Aren't you going to wear it at the trials?" asked Jessie.

"I don't know what I'm going to do with it," said Dara. "I don't feel right just ignoring Mother's present but I do wish she hadn't given it to me."

"Well, I say we go decide in the nearest pizza parlor," said Kate, closing Night Owl's door behind him.

"Pizza!" sighed Dara. "Imagine, warm, fresh-made pizza with extra sauce and cheese ..."

"And pepperoni," chimed in Jessie.

"And onions and green peppers," Kate added and laughed. "I'll go see if Casey wants to come."

She found Casey in the tack room.

"Hey, Case, want to break out of this place with us?" she asked. "We've got a car and we're headed into Mansfield to do some serious pizza eating."

Casey laughed. "Gosh, I'd really love to, but Trevor and I are going to coach each other on the outside course."

Kate felt her stomach drop, but she managed to keep smiling. "Oh ... okay. Maybe some other time. Jessie's here all week."

"Great," enthused Casey, but Kate could tell that the excitement glowing in her eyes wasn't for pepperoni and mushrooms.

"Catch you later," said Kate, backing out of the tack room. "Have a good workout."

"Thanks," said Casey.

Kate and Dara changed in two minutes flat and in another three the girls had loaded up the posters and were headed back down the valley toward Mansfield, the nearest town. The wind whipped in the open windows and the sun danced in and out of the building clouds, sprinkling the road in front of them with yellow patches.

"I feel like I've been released from prison," Kate said and sighed, forcing thoughts of Casey and Trevor out of her mind. What did she care for, anyway? She'd rejected Trevor. Why couldn't he and Casey become interested in each other?

"I must admit this does feel pretty good," said Dara. She turned to Jessie. "So, Jess, how are things going with Amory? You haven't said a word about him."

Jessie broke into a big grin. "Fine. We've been having a great summer. He comes out and helps me with my chores at the farm when he gets a chance."

"Lucky Jessie," moaned Dara. "You get a boyfriend who's at least trying to understand your world."

"Won't you miss him?" asked Kate. "I mean, being up here all this week."

"Sure I will," said Jessie. "I already do and I've only been gone one day. Did I tell you that he's been accepted at MIT for next year? So, he's working hard to help pay his tuition. In between all our jobs, we get together when we can and have a wonderful time."

Kate looked at Dara. "Why does it all sound so simple when Jessie explains it?"

"Because Jessie has her head screwed on right and you and I haven't," teased Dara, then she asked more somberly, "Have you ... uh ... seen Doug at all this summer?"

"Once," said Jessie. "At Lickety Split. He was ordering a double banana split with ... let me see ... ah yes, butter pecan ... and—"

"Jessie!" cried Dara. "I don't care what he was eating. Was he with anyone?"

"Sure," said Jessie, smiling wickedly.

Dara slumped down in the seat dejectedly.

"Silly, he was with Sean Pinell, his doubles partner," said Jessie. "They'd just won the quarterfinals at the club tournament."

Dara laughed. "I guess I'm getting a little paranoid, huh?" she said.

"From what I read in the papers, all he's done all summer is play tennis," said Jessie. "Good tennis. He keeps winning."

Dara smiled proudly. "I can't wait to see him play again. He's so wonderful to watch."

"Uh ... how about Pete?" said Kate hesitantly. "Has he been around?"

"Pete? Pete who?" teased Jessie. "Oh, you mean that tall guy with the blond hair and the terrific smile."

"Jessie, don't torture me," cried Kate. "Just give me the scoop."

"As a matter of fact I did see him," said Jessie.

"When? Where?" said Kate, grabbing Jessie's arm.

"He came out to the farm last week."

"Windcroft? To see me?" asked Kate. "He must have thought I would be home by now."

"Actually he came to deliver five hundred pounds of shelled corn. You know he's working at the feed store this summer, don't you?" said Jessie.

"Oh, right. I'd forgotten," said Kate with disappointment.

"However, he did mention that he'd gotten a letter from you," continued Jessie.

"Yeah? What else did he say?" said Kate eagerly.

" 'Are you authorized to sign for this grain, Miss Robeson,' " said Jessie in a deep voice, then added, "At least I think that's how he put it."

"You're terrible." But Kate giggled in spite of herself.

"Well, here we are in mighty Mansfield," announced Dara. "The original one-light town."

"We better hurry up and get these posters out," said Kate, scanning the sky. The clouds were gathering in thick black wads over the mountaintops. "Looks like we're in for a pretty big storm."

"Hey, there's our pizza!" cried Jessie, pointing to a flashing neon sign in the only cafe on the strip.

"Let's offer them our first poster," suggested Dara.

"Charge!" said Kate, scrambling from the car with a load of posters under her arm.

Chapter 11

AT the first crack of thunder, Kate sat bolt upright in bed. Almost immediately lightning bleached the room, and the thunder rolled through again, renewed, angrier than before. The whole room shook. Outside the trees raked their limbs back and forth across the sky as if imploring the heavens for mercy. Kate watched with fascinated horror, remembering the storm she and Dara had met with their first day in Vermont. It wasn't nearly as bad as this.

"Kate! What? ... Who? ..." Dara stumbled from her bed, still wrapped in her blankets, and plopped down beside Kate. They looked out the window together.

"Wow! This is some kind of wild storm," said Dara sleepily.

"You're not kidding," Kate replied. "Look at those trees. The branches look like they could snap off any minute."

99

"I guess the horses will be all right," said Dara, wrapping her blankets up tight under her chin.

"Sure. That old barn has probably stood there for two hundred years," Kate said reassuringly. "I doubt if this little storm is going to take it out now."

"I hope not."

Just then their door flew open and in shot Casey. She tripped over Jessie's cot and fell on a heap beside them.

"I'm scared," she said.

"And I'm tired," said Jessie from beneath her covers. "Don't you guys ever sleep in this place?"

"Jess, wake up!" said Kate. "Come watch this storm with us. It's wild. Looks like the lightning is hitting the ground right in front of us."

Jessie staggered over to Kate's bed and joined the others.

"Wow!" she said in awe. "This is a major light show. Look at that stuff."

"Yeah, I'd say we're in the eye of the storm," said Kate. "See how close together the thunder and lightning come."

They all watched and listened in silence. Lightning ripped the night into blackened shreds. Thunder pounded the world with its mighty blows. Then suddenly the wind flung a sheet of rain at the window.

"Uh-oh," said Kate, jumping from the bed and slamming the window shut. It rattled in protest as millions of raindrops smashed against it. "Here comes the rain."

The world outside looked even eerier through the wash of rain—distorted and weird and ghostly.

"What's that light over there?" asked Casey, as she strained to see through the rain-stained window.

"Where?" said the others, crowding up close.

"There, where the barn is," Casey said, her voice rising in alarm.

"I see it! I see it!" cried Jessie. "It's flickering. No, it's getting bigger. What? . . ."

"Fire!" yelled Kate, instinctively pulling on her sneakers. "The barn's on fire!"

"No!" screamed Dara in disbelief. "No! The horses!"

The girls scrambled for the door, yelling to wake the others. People staggered out of their rooms, wild-eyed, some half-asleep, others fully awake.

"The barn's on fire!" screamed Kate, racing down the stairs. "Jess, call the fire department! The phone's right here! Dara, Casey, come with me! Hurry! *Hurry!*"

Once outside, the blast of cold rain shocked Kate into full awareness. Now she could clearly see the tongues of red and orange flames flicking the low, dark clouds. She could hear the loud, terrified cries of the horses between the moans of thunder. Her heart pounded painfully as she raced toward the stables, her sneakers slipping and sliding on the wet grass. The others were right behind. She grabbed the big front door of the barn and tried to slide it open, but the wind pushed against it, resisting her. Suddenly Trevor was beside her. Together they yanked and tugged until the door slid free. Smoke rolled out in a thick ball, choking them, stinging their eyes. Then, it seemed to Kate as if time actually stood still for a moment. Instinctively everyone moved to their own horse's stable as if taking part in a well-rehearsed dance, reaching out as they did for the lead shank and towel they knew would be hanging beside the door.

The door to Night Owl's stall opened smoothly, without protest. She could see his white, frightened eyes in the dark as he swung his huge body nervously back and forth. Above them the fire crackled and popped ominously, sending down showers of sparks and burning cinders.

"Hang on, Big Bird," said Kate, forcing herself to speak slowly and calmly while she patted his nose. "It's going to be okay. Everything's all right."

She attached the lead shank to his halter and, after rubbing the towel over his face briefly so he'd know its feel and smell, she tied it across his eyes, all the while talking and clucking to him. Almost immediately she could feel him relax a bit. Still talking in low, reassuring tones, she opened his door wide and led him out into the center aisle. The other horses were being led out, too. Some pranced gingerly, some snorted loudly, others whinnied continuously—a high, piercing noise of utter terror—but in the end they all gave themselves up to their owners' commands. All except the Robber Baron. After an initial fight, Caroline had managed to get the lead shank on him, but he refused to let her wrap his eyes. And, when she tried to get him to follow her out unwrapped, he reared back from her and circled nervously on the short rope. Caroline, hysteria distorting her pale face, pleaded with him, but it only distressed him more. He plunged and circled and pulled, his eyes rolling back in his head, his nostrils flaring. His antics upset the other horses trying to move past him.

"Easy, Bird, easy now," cooed Kate, trying to keep the fear out of her voice as she coaxed her horse around the Baron. She could see the open door flash occasionally through the swirling smoke and tried to head straight for it, but the thick atmosphere and the screaming horses distorted everything—sight, hearing, smell, taste. The lead shank felt clammy in her sweaty hands. Onward they plunged, knocking into other people and horses. And then, suddenly, the barn door loomed before them—a great black hole, but before she could reach it a large, burning beam dropped from above onto Night Owl's leg. The smell of burning hair filled Kate's nose and her stomach heaved with sickness. She kicked the beam away and led him quickly around it and out of the barn.

For a second she couldn't move as she gulped lungful after lungful of sweet, delicious air. Fire trucks screaming up the driveway snapped Kate back into action. She had to get help for Caroline! She searched the tangled group of people and horses for Dara and Casey. They were standing together, their arms around their horses' necks, tears of joy and relief filling their eyes. Some were sobbing out loud. Kate felt her own throat catch when she pulled the blind off Night Owl. He looked so afraid, the whites of his eyes still showing all around. He glanced around wildly. Kate put one hand reassuringly on his neck and led him over to her friends.

"Casey!" croaked Kate, her parched throat reluctant to strain itself further. "You've got to come back in with me."

"Wha ... what! Why?" stammered Casey as Kate dissolved into racking coughs.

"It's Caroline," spat out Kate. "She can't get the Baron out. You've got to help."

Jessie ran up. Her face was white with fear, but her expression eased when she saw that Kate and Dara were safe.

"Jess, hold Night Owl and take a look at his wound," said Kate, handing Jessie the lead shank. "Dara, can you handle Casey's horse, too?"

Dara nodded.

"Great," said Kate. "Come on, Case! Quick! We haven't much time. The top of the barn is starting to collapse."

Kate wished more than anything she didn't have to go back into that barn. She was too aware of the dangers. She'd seen them firsthand and realized that her life was in serious danger. The two girls raced around the firemen who were blasting the barn with streams of water.

"We're bringing another horse out," shouted Kate. "Keep the water back for a minute."

The firemen nodded and redirected the spray to the roof.

Inside the smoke was even thicker, the air more difficult to breathe. It tortured Kate's raw throat. They headed straight for the Baron's stall. Caroline, her face blackened with smoke and streaked with tears, was still wrestling with her horse. The Baron was dripping with the sweat of unrestrained terror.

"Caroline," said Kate sharply, realizing the girl was ready to collapse from fear herself, "leave him to Casey."

Caroline looked at her wild-eyed, her hand clenched tightly to the lead shank. Kate put her arm around Caroline's shoulders.

"It's all right," she said reassuringly. "I'm taking you out. Casey can handle the Baron. Give the lead shank to Casey."

Still Caroline hesitated. Kate's heart pounded. The three of them were the only ones in the barn now and the fire was a steady roar above them. Lighted cinders fell·in showers around them. She glanced at Casey, who was talking softly to Caroline's horse. Kate could see that he was responding, but they didn't have much time. Suddenly, with a great roar of defiance, the back section of the barn fell, sending a hurricane of scalding air over them. Kate knew she couldn't hesitate a moment longer. Gently but firmly she unwound Caroline's fingers from the lead shank and handed it to Casey. Casey expertly wrapped the towel over the Baron's eyes and, talking to him the whole while, began to lead him out. He moved gingerly, still unsure, shying every time a cinder popped or crackled. But he followed Casey, and finally Caroline let Kate lead her out, too.

The first thing Kate heard when they got outside was Langwald's voice, shouting reassurance to everyone over the frenzy of the fire. People stood numbly beside their horses well back from the blaze, listening to him, their expressionless faces reflecting the shock of the experience.

"Okay," said Langwald calmly. "I'm pretty sure we're all here. But let me just call roll to be sure."

There was a "here," sometimes not very loud, sometimes choked with tears, to every name he called out. Three more fire trucks raced up the drive and jockeyed for position beside the burning building. The fire hissed violently as the torrents of water blasted it.

"Now then," he continued. "Move your horses away from this area as quickly and calmly as you can. Let the firemen do their job. Find stalls for your horses—anything will do for tonight—in the barn behind the house and make them comfortable. Give them a scoop of grain and be sure they have plenty of water. They're probably pretty dehydrated after all this. Then all meet in the kitchen for a cup of hot chocolate. It's been a pretty rugged night, but you all performed marvelously. I'm very proud of you."

Kate took Night Owl's lead from Jessie. The gash in his leg had stopped bleeding and didn't look too serious. She dabbed at it with her towel and patted his head. For a long while she just stared into his deep brown, trusting eyes. Then suddenly she burst into tears.

"He could have been killed," she sobbed, laying her head on his neck. "He could have been killed."

Dara put her arm around Kate and hugged her closely. Kate looked at her friend. Tears streamed down her face, too. They clung to each other, overwhelmed by the immensity of what they'd just escaped.

Before leading their horses away, they turned to watch the fire. The firemen obviously had it under control. The flames were almost gone. Only one end of the barn—the stall section—had burned. The tack room and granary were saved. The storm had passed now, too, leaving behind a steady but gentle rain.

An unnatural calm enshrouded the ragtag group as they led their horses over to their new home.

"Casey, Kate," said Caroline, leading the Baron up to the group. "I ... I want to thank you."

"Hey, don't mention it," said Casey lightly. "You'd have saved old Peapod here, I'm sure."

"I don't really mean that," said Caroline quietly. "Although, naturally, I'm eternally grateful that you saved my horse."

They all pulled their horses to a halt and stared at Caroline. Her silk pajamas were torn and smeared with grime. Her wet hair was plastered to her head. The revolving lights from the fire trucks washed her face in unnatural red, then yellow light, making her eyes glow brightly. Caroline just looked at them without speaking for a while. Kate wondered if she was in shock or something.

"No," said Caroline finally. "I want to thank you for showing me friendship."

They all continued to stare, not knowing what to say. Everything was so weird this evening.

"I know I've been difficult to be around," continued Caroline in the same quiet voice. "I didn't want to be. I was just so ... scared."

"Scared?" said Kate. "Of what?"

"You. All of you." Caroline stared at her feet as she talked. "You all made friends so easily. I

envied you. I wanted to sit in the rec room with
my feet up, sharing secrets and stuff."

"But you never even came in the place," said
Casey, confused.

"I didn't know how to," whispered Caroline.

"Just open the door and walk on in," said Kate.

Caroline laughed a little. "That's so easy for
you, but I was just too scared." She hesitated,
then added, "My mother has always told me how
different and better I am than everybody. I always
knew inside that I wasn't so special. I didn't even
want to be. I wanted to be like everyone else but
she wouldn't let me. Always organizing my life—
what I would do, who I could know."

Dara had been standing off to the side listening. Now she had to say something. "I think I
know exactly what you mean," she shared with
Caroline, "My mother's the same way."

"She is?" said Caroline in surprise.

"Exactly," said Dara.

"But, you're so nice and normal," protested
Caroline.

"Ha!" said Kate and Jessie, teasingly. "We know
better."

Dara laughed. "See, they'll tell you how horrible I can be."

"And Dara will tell you how horrible I can be,"
tossed out Kate with a giggle.

"And Kate will tell you how horrible I can be."
Jessie laughed.

Soon they were all laughing, a little extra loud,
a little too long in an effort to replace the fears of
the night.

"You mean, you guys can really fight and then

make up and everything's okay?" Caroline asked incredulously.

"Sure," said Kate. "Keeps life exciting."

"Wow!" Caroline stared at them all in disbelief. Then she turned to Casey. "I've always wanted to be your friend. You are one of the nicest people I know."

"Geez," said Casey, her face going bright red. "Thanks."

"No ... thank you," said Caroline. "You taught me a pretty important lesson here tonight."

"I don't know if I can take anymore," said Casey with a laugh.

"Well, you've got to," said Caroline. "Getting the Baron out of the fire like that made me really understand what trust is all about. He trusted you because you're the one who looks after him ... who really cares about him."

"That's important," said Casey seriously. "To perform well, your horse has to trust you. He has to be your friend."

"I only just understood that ... tonight," said Caroline. Suddenly she grinned. "So, you're fired as my groom!"

Everyone laughed.

"Let's get these poor horses settled down for the night," said Kate finally.

"Poor horses?" said Casey. "Poor us. I may just need an extra fix of chocolate to get me over this trauma."

Caroline laughed.

"What a night it's been." Dara sighed. "I'm sure glad no more damage was done."

"Yeah," agreed Jessie. "Things looked pretty hairy there for a while."

Most of the other horses had been put up when the girls led theirs in.

"I guess it's every person for herself," said Kate, walking down the aisle looking for an empty stall. Suddenly she stopped and stared hard through the bars of a stall. "Dara!" she whispered loudly. "Come here! Quick!"

Dara joined her immediately and they both stared at the horse within. She was almost the same pale color as the fresh straw she lay asleep on. Her mane and tail were snow white.

"It's her!" Kate whispered hoarsely. "Elsinore of Bodiam!"

"Wow!" breathed Dara.

"Can you believe it?" gasped Kate.

"She's beautiful," sighed Dara. "Absolutely beautiful."

Chapter 12

"WELL, Big Bird," Kate said as she pulled the last bit of bandage off Night Owl's cut, "I don't think it's going to keep you out of the competition tomorrow." She gently prodded the area around the wound. It was almost a week old now. Night Owl didn't flinch. "Yep, it's looking pretty good." She opened a jar of salve and began to dab it on the scab. Night Owl continued to munch his hay contentedly.

"How's he doing?"

Kate looked up, startled by the familiar voice. Trevor was leaning on the door of the stall staring down at her.

"Uh ... he ... he's fine, thanks," stammered Kate. This was the first time she'd really been alone with Trevor since their moonlight ride. She felt embarrassed all over again for rejecting him that night, but what else could she have done? Seeing him so close now, though, she felt a rush

111

of warm emotion. She'd really missed him these past two weeks.

"Are you going to invite me in, or shall I just shout from here?" Trevor asked, flashing his friendliest grin.

"Oh ... no ... come in," Kate said, jumping to her feet and unlatching the door. She wondered what in the world Trevor wanted. "Come in."

Night Owl turned his head to see what all the commotion was about, then went back to his food. Trevor patted his back.

"I didn't sleep much last night, Kate," began Trevor, nervously picking at pieces of straw caught in Night Owl's coat.

"Yeah, I think the trials have got everyone a little wired around here," Kate said. She grabbed her curry comb and began furiously grooming Night Owl.

"No ... no, it isn't the trials," said Trevor. "Not really. I mean ..."

Kate scrubbed Night Owl harder and harder. He flicked his tail in annoyance. She patted him by way of apology and switched to a softer brush.

"I just lay awake a long time ... thinking," began Trevor. "The day after tomorrow we all split." He stared at her across Night Owl's back. "We've had some good times this summer ... at least in the beginning."

"Yeah," Kate said, then laughed nervously. "Mucking out stalls ain't what it used to be."

Trevor laughed, too, and kicked at the straw bedding with his foot. Suddenly he got serious again.

"I tried ... hard ... to forget about you after our ride that night. I mean, I was really hurting, Kate."

"I'm sorry, Trevor," began Kate, her face wrinkled with concern. "I ..."

"Naw, don't be sorry," Trevor said. "I'm the one who should apologize. I've been the jerk. You offered me friendship and I rejected it."

They stood staring at each other across Night Owl's back.

"I'd like to accept that offer if it's still available," Trevor finally said.

Kate didn't trust herself to talk, her heart was so full of emotion, so she just nodded.

"Then, we can still be friends?" asked Trevor.

"I hope forever," said Kate. "You're the brother I never had."

"Well, I have a sister," laughed Trevor with relief, "but I'd trade her in for you any day."

Kate giggled. "I don't think you can do that."

"I'm willing to try," said Trevor, grinning from ear to ear. "Now then, if I don't get saddled up and out in that ring, I'll never be able to beat you tomorrow."

"Beat me!" Kate laughed. "Never. Night Owl and I are going to walk off with all the ribbons. Watch out!"

Trevor laughed as he opened the stall door and stepped out. He hesitated a moment, then looked back at Kate. "Thanks, Kate," he said.

"Don't thank me," said Kate. "Just save me a place in the dessert line tonight."

"It's yours," shot back Trevor, then headed down the aisle, whistling away.

*   *   *

"Here I am, Robber Baron, ready to groom you until you gleam."

Kate recognized Caroline's voice and came to the door of Night Owl's stall. "You've certainly made great progress this week," she said laughingly.

"Thanks," Caroline shouted back.

Just then Dara came out of Arpeggio's stall and wandered over to Kate. They watched Caroline struggle, carrying her assortment of grooming brushes to where the Baron was standing tied to a cross-tie.

"Looks like Caroline really has changed," said Kate.

"Yeah, I think so," said Dara. "She and I stayed up talking for a long time after the fire. It's wild, but our mothers sound like twins. We've agreed to stay in touch, sort of a Daughters-of-Pushy-Moms support group."

Kate laughed. "Funny how things often aren't what they seem."

"Like what?" asked Dara.

"Like Caroline for instance. We've been around her all these weeks and never knew what a nice person she could be." Night Owl had finished eating. He came up behind Kate and rested his head on her shoulder. Kate rubbed his ear absentmindedly.

"Well, she didn't make it very easy for us, you've got to admit," Dara said.

"That's true, nor did Langwald," said Kate.

"Are you going to start in on him again?" Dara sighed.

"No, I'm actually going to give him a compliment."

Dara faked a faint against the stall door. Kate laughed.

"Don't worry, I didn't say I was signing up to be president of the Tommy Fangwald Fan Club," Kate said, then added gravely, "but thanks to his neurotic organization, we all got our horses safely out of the fire."

"That's true," said Dara. "I actually thought about that the night of the fire. I went into that burning barn feeling pretty calm, because I knew everything would be where it was supposed to be."

"Yeah, me too," admitted Kate. "I think I could have saved Night Owl with my eyes closed. I mean, how many times have we all checked to be sure the lead lines were in place beside those towels."

Dara started laughing. "Remember how you ranted and moaned about oiling the hinges on the doors?"

"Okay, okay." Kate laughed. "I admit it now—it was a good idea. A great idea!"

The two girls turned and watched Caroline cluck and coo to the Baron as she brushed him from top to tail.

"Gosh, it feels like we've been at this place half our lives," said Dara finally.

"Yeah. Probably just because we've aged so much from overwork," joked Kate, scratching Night Owl's chin.

"Well, I for one have gotten a lot out of it," said Dara.

"I'll give you my report after the trials tomorrow," Kate said. "At least Fangwald won't be a judge so maybe I have half a chance."

"I'm glad Jessie's here," added Dara. "It'll be nice to have a fan cheering us on."

"Where is Jess, by the way?" asked Kate.

"She told me she was going to try to catch up on some sleep, then she had some things to do."

"Things to do? Like what?" asked Kate.

"I don't know. That's just what she said. Said she'd see us for dinner."

"Hmmm," mused Kate. "I wonder what she's up to."

"Well, I better be up to some pretty fancy jumping if I'm going to beat you tomorrow," teased Dara, starting to walk away.

"It won't happen," challenged Kate, not feeling nearly as confident as she sounded.

"Hey ... what was that noise?" said Dara, suddenly stopping in her tracks.

"What noise?" asked Kate.

"I don't know, it was just weird," said Dara. "Listen! There it is again."

"It's a horse," said Kate. "But it does sound weird. We better check it out."

The girls walked quickly down the aisle, glancing into all the stalls.

"Look," cried Kate. "It's Casey! She's out cold!"

Caroline ran up as they pulled open Sweetpea's stall door. Lying in the hay at their feet was Casey, but her face was pale and her cheeks were sunken. Sweetpea was nosing around her, nickering in distress.

"Dr. Andrews is here," said Caroline, her face wreathed in concern. "I saw him come in a little while ago. He's seeing to that palomino, I think."

"I'll get him," said Kate, already running to the door.

Dr. Andrews and Langwald were bent over Elsinore. Her sides were heaving as if breathing was almost impossible. Kate hardly noticed.

"Dr. Andrews! Mr. Langwald! Come quickly! It's Casey! She's fainted or something! Quick! She's in Sweetpea's stall."

The two men were right on Kate's heels as she sped back. Caroline was sitting on the hay next to Casey, holding her hand.

"Her pulse seems awfully fast," said Caroline, her eyes brimming with tears.

Dr. Andrews knelt down beside Casey, looked her over, then pulled a bottle from his bag. It was liniment for horses' strained muscles and had a strong, acrid odor. He opened it and stuck it under Casey's nose. In a few seconds Casey coughed and spluttered, then opened her eyes.

"Casey," said Dr. Andrews very calmly. "Are you all right?"

"Yes ... yes ... I think so," stammered Casey, struggling to sit up. Everyone reached out to help her at once.

"Can you tell me what happened?" continued the doctor.

"I was ... I was grooming the Pod here," said Casey, rubbing her horse's nose. "And then I don't know what happened. I don't remember."

"Lie back," ordered the doctor.

When Casey was lying flat in the hay, Dr. Andrews pulled up her large T-shirt and began poking her stomach. Kate and Dara glanced at each other. Casey's ribs were sticking out all over the place. She always buried herself in such baggy shirts, they hadn't noticed how skinny she had gotten.

"Casey, have you been eating?" asked Kate.

"No," Casey proudly announced, looking at Langwald. "I've learned discipline. I've even managed not to eat a thing for three whole days."

Langwald groaned. "Casey," he said, and Kate was surprised to hear such tenderness in his voice. "The idea was just to get your eating under control, not starve yourself to death."

"I wanted to be in a size five coat for the trials tomorrow," said Casey. "I've still got to get to town to buy it."

"You're not going anywhere, young lady," said Dr. Andrews. "If you plan to be competing tomorrow, you're going to spend the rest of the day in bed—eating. I don't think you've done any major damage. You're just weak and dehydrated." He turned to Langwald. "When I get to town I'll send Dr. Taylor out to check her over."

"Okay, young lady, off you go," ordered the doctor. "To bed with you."

"But, my horse!" protested Casey.

"What about your horse?" asked Dr. Andrews.

"I've got to get her ready for the trials tomorrow," said Casey, close to tears. "She needs a bath."

"I'll do it," said Caroline. "You just get to bed and get better."

"And I'll saddle-soap your saddle," said Kate.

Dara chimed in, "And since I'm the best manebraider this side ..." She turned to Langwald. "What's the name of that river out there?"

"Devil's Run," he said.

"This side of Devil's Run," continued Dara, "I'll take care of that."

Casey smiled weakly at them. "Thanks, guys."

Caroline and Dara watched Langwald help Casey back to the house, then returned to their horses. Kate stayed behind with Dr. Andrews, who was putting things back in his bag.

"Dr. Andrews," asked Kate. "What's wrong with that palomino you've been treating?"

"Ellie?" he said.

"Is that what you call her?" Kate said.

"That's what Mr. Langwald calls her. It's his horse. Elsinore of Bodiam. But he's always called her Ellie. Leastways, as long as I've known the two of them and that's going on fifteen years."

"She must be pretty old then," said Kate.

"She'll be twenty-three end of this summer."

"Wow, she sure doesn't look that old," Kate said.

"No ... no, she doesn't. She's always had a special quality about her."

Kate thought of how Ellie's picture had mesmerized her from the first. "Is she Lang ... Mr. Langwald's favorite horse or something?"

Dr. Andrews looked at her for a long moment. "That horse is the reason Tommy Langwald didn't make the Olympic team."

Kate stared at him in confusion.

"He loved ... loves ... that horse. Everyone told him she wasn't Olympic material, but he just couldn't—or maybe wouldn't—believe it. He gave up fame for her. He was an outstanding rider."

"Wow ..." said Kate in awe and confusion. The Langwald she knew and the Langwald she was hearing about now just didn't sound like the same person.

"Yep," continued Dr. Andrews. "Old Tommy was Olympic material all right. Let his feelings get in the way though."

Dr. Andrews snapped his bag shut. "Can't fault him on it. It was his own decision."

Chapter 13

KATE pulled the brush along Night Owl's side. His smooth coat glowed a rich mahogany. His tail and mane looked like black silk. She knew there wasn't a single bit of dust or dirt on him, but the mindless activity helped her keep her breakfast down. She was a bundle of nerves. Maybe it was her dream last night. . . .

She'd been in a huge ring. It was foggy and the jumps appeared and disappeared around her like ghosts on a moonless night. She tried to remember the course description but Langwald's voice came booming out of the fog, finding fault with her every move: "Rounder, you've got to get him rounder, get him on the bit, more action in the hindquarters, wake him up. For heaven's sake—wake him up!" She'd woken in a sweat and hadn't been able to get back to sleep after that.

Kate glanced at Dara, who was putting the finishing touches on Arpeggio. She looked cool, calm and collected. As usual on the morning of horse trials, she and Dara went their separate ways. As friends they didn't like the idea of competing against one another; especially since they were so evenly matched. But as two people who spent most of their waking hours preparing for such moments as this day, each was eager for the chance to prove herself.

Kate looked around for Jessie. Where was she? She said she'd be here. Calm down, kid, Kate told herself. You've been in much bigger competitions before. This is really a dinky little event.

She lowered the saddle gently on Night Owl's back. There was a silent but vibrant energy all around her in the barn as her fellow students prepared for the day's events. She knew they were all eyeing each other. She glanced at her watch. The dressage test began in less than an hour. Then there would be the cross-country and probably the stadium jumping after lunch. The butterflies in Kate's stomach took flight. She slipped Night Owl's halter off and put on his bridle.

"Well, Bird, you certainly look like a champion," said Kate, taking a step back and checking him out. His eyes were bright and his ears perked forward. Kate put her arms around his neck. "You know something's up, don't you, old boy? Well, all I ask is that you take this very seriously. We've got to prove to Langwald once and for all that we're champs, right?" Night Owl nuzzled his nose into her shoulder.

"The Bird looks great today," said Casey, walking Sweetpea by.

"So does the Pod," remarked Kate.

"Thanks to you guys," said Casey.

"How are you feeling?" asked Kate.

"Terrific," Casey said, then laughed. "Scared, but terrific. Just wish I had myself tucked into a sassy little size five jacket." Her old jacket was baggy and ill-fitting now that she'd lost so much weight.

Kate laughed. "I'll see you out there in a few minutes."

Kate yanked off her sweatshirt that had been protecting her white eventing shirt beneath and slipped into her black tailored jacket. She gave her boots a final swipe with the towel. They shone a deep, rich ebony. Finally, she smoothed her hair down with her hand and set her hard hat squarely on her head.

"Okay, Big Bird," she said, taking a deep breath. "We're as ready as we'll ever be."

Kate sucked in her breath again when she exited from the barn. The parking lot was backed up with cars and more were pouring into the field across the road. People were streaming toward the eventing area with blankets and picnic baskets and sun hats and coolers.

"My gosh!" said Dara, coming up behind her. "I never expected to see so many people."

"Me neither," Kate said. More than ever she wished her parents were there. Never had she been in a show without at least one of them there, fussing over her, helping her with all the last-minute bits and pieces.

"Casey told me it's the biggest event of the

summer around here," said Trevor, leading Paint-Patch by. "She said people come from all over southern Vermont to watch."

Trevor stopped right in front of her and smiled warmly. "Good luck today, Kate."

"Yeah, you, too," said Kate, then added teasingly, "Just don't expect to steal any ribbons from me."

Trevor laughed. "We'll see."

"Well, I guess we ought to get warmed up," said Dara, pulling herself up onto Arpeggio's back. The thoroughbred accepted her weight calmly and waited for her signal to proceed. Night Owl was too busy looking around and started to walk off when Kate put her foot in the stirrup.

"Whoa!" snapped Kate. "Stand still."

"Want me to wait for you?" asked Dara.

"No," said Kate. "We need to work out our bugs alone. Thanks anyway."

Kate felt sick watching Dara and Arpeggio wander calmly off. It was this calmness that won ribbons. She got up on Night Owl, dropped her legs from the stirrups, closed her eyes and breathed deeply for several minutes. She felt some of the tension leave her back, then she headed for the ring. Coming around the far side of the barn, the trials area opened up before her, full of horses and people and excitement. Night Owl and Kate took it all in. If only she saw the familiar blue Chevy and her dad's good luck crossed-fingers signal to her. But all she saw was a sea of strangers. And ... Jessie!

"Hi!" said Jessie cheerfully, running up. "How are you feeling?"

"A little nervous," admitted Kate. "This is kind of my last chance to prove myself to Langwald."

"Forget Langwald," Jessie said.

"Forget Langwald? Forget that I exist maybe!" Kate said. "Where have you been anyway?"

"Arranging a little surprise for you." Jessie grinned mischievously. "Follow me."

Kate couldn't imagine what Jessie was up to but followed her obediently. Jessie motioned for Dara to join them. Suddenly the door of a car opened and a familiar face emerged.

"Pete!" cried Kate, not realizing until that very minute how much she'd really missed him.

He grinned at her and opened his arms. Kate slid off Night Owl and into his hug.

"What? ... How? ..." she stammered, then laughed. "This is great! How'd you get here?"

"Came up with Amory," said Pete.

"He's here!" cried Kate.

"Sure am," Amory said. He was standing on the other side of the car with his arm around Jessie. Jessie was grinning like the Cheshire cat.

"How about Doug?" asked Kate.

"Uh ... we invited him, but he couldn't make it," Pete replied, turning to Dara who rode up on Arpeggio. "He wanted to. He really did. But he made it to the finals in the tennis tournament so he had to play today and tomorrow."

Kate could see Dara's shoulders sag, and her heart went out to her friend.

"Oh well," said Dara. "I'll see him tomorrow. It's good to have the rest of you guys up here, I tell you. We need a fan club. There are some amazing riders in this bunch, so don't expect us to be the highest scorers. Just cheer us on."

"We're here for you, win or lose," Pete said and grinned broadly.

The silver bell, announcing the first competitor in the dressage test, rang out. Kate's heart jumped in anticipation. She was the sixth competitor so she had a little bit more time before she had to mount up.

Pete suddenly held Kate away from him. His blue eyes twinkled and the sun threw yellow sparkles through his sandy hair. "You look great, Kate. I've missed you."

"I've missed you, too," she admitted, "but you could have called or written or something."

Pete dropped his hands to his sides and concentrated on his feet for a second. "Well, I guess I got a little ticked off when you didn't even call to say good-bye." He shifted his weight from one foot to the other. "I mean ... I sent you a rose and everything. I never did anything like that before."

"But ... but I did call!" protested Kate in disbelief. "Just before we left for Vermont."

"You couldn't have. I was home," said Pete with equal incredulity. "And the phone's right by my bed."

"I know," countered Kate. "I woke you up. You even told me you'd been working till ten o'clock the night before."

"Oh wow!" exclaimed Pete, throwing an arm around her shoulders. "You did call. I remember now. Wow! I must have really been into some heavy-duty sleeping."

"You were," Kate said, then laughed. "You sounded like you were on Mars."

Pete laughed, too. "One thing you'll have to learn about me," he said. "I take my sleeping very seriously."

"Yeah," retorted Kate teasingly. "You and the bears. You sounded like you were coming out of a three-month hibernation or something. Not exactly pleasant."

"Well," Pete grinned wickedly at her, "I'm being pleasant now, aren't I?"

"Yeah," admitted Kate. "But how come you never answered my letter?"

Pete stepped back and spread his arms wide. "I'm here. That's your answer. I wanted to surprise you."

Kate giggled as she wrapped her arms around him. He felt warm and sunny. "Okay. Okay. I forgive you."

The tinkle of the bell announced the next competitor. Kate swallowed hard. It was time to get serious.

"We better get over to the course," said Dara.

Kate gave Pete a final squeeze and climbed up on Night Owl.

"Oh, Kate," said Jessie, coming around the side of the car. "I almost forgot. These are for you. From your mom and dad."

Kate took the little box and opened it carefully. Tears blinded her. Lying on a bed of dried rose petals was the little gold horseshoe her dad had given her before her first show when she was six, and beside it was a little gold unicorn. Kate knew this was from her mother because they had both always loved the enchanting, mythical creature. Kate fastened one pin under each lapel and poured the rose petals into her pocket. Her heart was full to bursting. She felt calm and confident and happy. Bring on the competition, she thought, taking up her reins. I'm ready. Night Owl responded to this new mood, listening attentively for her every signal.

Caroline was in the dressage arena when Kate and Dara rode up. They paused to watch.

"Wow," said Kate. "They're actually working together. Look."

"Unbelievable," agreed Dara. "I mean, it's not total harmony yet, but you can see they're headed for it. Caroline's really a superb rider."

"We'll be up soon," said Kate. "I'm going to get the Owl moving."

"Good idea," said Dara.

They rode off in opposite directions, but stayed close to the entrance gate so they could be nearby when their numbers were called.

"Number 44," the starter called out. "Number 44 please."

Casey! thought Kate, and paused in her warm-up. She almost didn't recognize her friend. Horse and rider were one sleek unit. No baggy T-shirts or coats billowing in the breeze. Casey had on a perfectly fitted midnight-blue jacket that showed to all the world that Casey O'Connell was exactly the right size for whatever she wanted to do in life.

Kate stared at the jacket. It looked so familiar. Suddenly it hit her. Dara! Dara had given Casey her new jacket. She sought out her friend. Their eyes met and they both gave the thumbs up.

Trevor went next and again Kate was compelled to watch. She knew he'd been working all week to get Paint-Patch's trot slowed down. She crossed her fingers for him now and said a little prayer. Her heart pounded, sharing the anxiety she knew he must be feeling. Paint-Patch performed like a champ.

"You looked terrific," said Kate when he exited the arena. "The trot was perfect."

Trevor grinned back. "I'll be watching you, too," he said.

Suddenly Kate realized she hadn't been thinking about winning so much. She wanted her friends to do well. And, after all, Pete was there. Her parents were thinking of her. No need to worry. Then, the starter announced Dara's number—number 36—and Kate felt her heart race anew. She walked Night Owl in a small, loose circle. She wanted to watch Dara and yet she didn't, so she settled for stolen glances every once in a while. After a couple though, she pulled Night Owl up and watched without breathing. Something was wrong. Dara usually sailed through these routines. But her actions looked labored now, as if her mind was somewhere else. She even signaled Arpeggio into a trot when it should have been a canter. Kate was concerned.

Dara glanced at her unhappily when she came out of the arena. Kate wished she could go up to her, but her own number had been called. She had ninety seconds to get into the arena. She took a deep breath, patted Night Owl quickly on the shoulder, and trotted in—back straight, head up, heart singing. She halted in front of the judges, took her reins in her left hand, dropped her right down by her side and bowed her head slightly. It was then, out of the corner of her eye that she saw Langwald. His expression seemed extra hard and serious, and Kate felt her confidence crack. Then she saw Pete. He winked at her, and the crack began to close.

When Kate came out of the arena five minutes later, she knew she and Night Owl had never performed so well. The routine had gone flawlessly. Kate turned triumphantly to Langwald but his chair was empty. She looked around for him, but he was nowhere in sight.

Chapter 14

"KATE!" shouted Pete rushing up. "You were terrific! Better than ever!" he enthused. He held Night Owl's reins while Kate dismounted. "I mean, I don't know much about all the finer points, but you seemed smoother or something."

Kate thought her grin was going to split her face. "Thanks," she said self-consciously.

"Yeah, this camp really has been good for you, hasn't it?" he said.

"Yeah, I guess so," said Kate, hating to admit it since she'd hated every minute of the camp. Or had she? She thought of her new friends—Caroline and Casey and Trevor, not to mention the others. She would see them again in the years ahead as they all competed at higher and higher levels. They might even compete against one another for a spot on the U.S. Equestrian Team, or someday maybe even the Olympics. But they would always have Langwald's as a bond between them. All his

relentless training and fanatical rules had forged
a bond that could never be broken.

Suddenly Kate was filled with emotion. She
hadn't wanted to leave home a month ago. She'd
been scared of being out on her own. But she'd
done it and it had worked. Now she felt sad about
leaving all her new friends tomorrow.

"Hey, shouldn't you get the saddle off this poor
old beast?" said Pete.

Kate snapped back to the present. "Good old
Bird. He deserves a rest. The cross-country won't
start for another hour."

Pete helped her untack Night Owl, rub the horse
down and settle him in his stall, then Kate took
him on a tour of the farm to use up the time until
the dressage scores were posted. She showed
him the main house and the stables, which still
smelled of burnt wood. He listened awestruck as
she told him about the fire. He laughed when she
told him about swimming with the horses in the
river. And he got very quiet when she told him
about Elsinore of Bodiam.

"Wow," he said solemnly. "Langwald must really love that horse to sacrifice his career for
her."

"Yeah," agreed Kate. "It's just hard to imagine
Langwald caring for anything. He's so hard-boiled."

Suddenly the loudspeaker crackled to life and
the announcement came that the cross-country
competition would commence in half an hour.

"I better go change and get the Bird," said Kate.

"Why don't I go get us a couple of hot dogs and
sodas from the concession stand?" said Pete.

"Great! I'm going to be starving after that cross-country course," said Kate, then added quietly, "I'm so glad you're here."

Pete put his arm around her. "Me, too."

"Can you stay for the cookout tonight?" asked Kate. "Langwald's giving us a farewell party."

"Sure. But Amory and I'll have to leave after that. We've got work tomorrow."

When Kate passed Arpeggio's stall, Dara was standing beside her horse, absentmindedly stroking his face.

"Dara?" said Kate.

"Yeah?"

"You okay?"

"Yeah."

Dara's voice was strained and her shoulders slumped.

"Want to warm up together?" Kate asked.

"Sure," Dara intoned.

When they'd tacked up, they met outside and walked their horses over to the warm-up area.

"Kate! Kate!" Casey came running over. "You won!"

Kate looked confused. "Won what?"

"The dressage, silly!" exclaimed Casey.

"Oh my gosh!" gushed Kate. "I forgot all about the scores." Her face turned red. "I was with Pete."

"Well, you won. You came in two whole points— ahead of me!" beamed Casey.

"You got second?" cried Kate.

"Yep," said Casey proudly.

"Case, that's wonderful!" said Kate. "Congratulations. You look really great, by the way."

Casey beamed. "Much as I hate to admit it, old Fangwald's discipline has done me some good. I really think I've got the eating thing under control for good now." She flashed a huge smile at Dara. "Of course, Dara's simply divine coat helps the old image considerably."

Kate laughed. "Who came in third?" she asked.

"Trevor," Casey answered, and avoided looking at Dara. She left quickly to share her good news with the others.

Kate and Dara started warming up their horses in silence. They took a couple of practice jumps in the field, and Kate could see that Dara was still distracted. Arpeggio performed like a glorious ship without a rudder. "Is it Doug, Dara?" asked Kate when they finally headed over to the start of the cross-country course.

"I guess so," said Dara. "I just wish he were here."

"I'm sorry he couldn't make it," said Kate sympathetically.

"I don't know what's going to happen to us," Dara burst out. "How can we have a relationship, if we can't even find time to be together?"

"It must be really hard," agreed Kate. She paused, then added, "But don't blow the trials today, Dara. Please. You've worked too hard for this."

"I don't really care," said Dara dejectedly. "I don't even feel like riding."

"Oh, Dara, please don't say that," begged Kate. "All the times I was moaning about Langwald, you were taking it all in and getting better and better. You deserve to do well today."

Dara looked at Kate's pleading face, then stared out over the fields.

"Do it for Arpeggio," continued Kate. "He's never let you down."

Just then Dara's number was called. Dara trotted Arpeggio toward the starting post without another word to Kate. The countdown began and then Dara was off. By the time Arpeggio rose like a magnificent gray wave to take the first obstacle, Kate knew Dara had snapped back. Her head was up, her back straight but supple. She and Arpeggio flowed over the jumps one after the other in perfect accord.

"Yahoo! Yippee!" shouted Kate when Dara crossed the line marking the end of the course. Dara trotted straight up to Kate and reined in. Her face was all smiles.

"Thanks ... friend," she said. "I needed that kick in the butt."

Kate laughed. "Yeah ... well ... I think I kicked myself out of a blue ribbon."

Now Dara laughed. "You can't have them all, you know."

"We'll see," teased Kate and headed off to the starting post as her number was called.

Kate almost couldn't wait to the end line before throwing her arms around Night Owl's neck. He'd done great. Maybe not as good as Arpeggio, but he'd really been on. He'd sailed over the assortment of obstacles—stone walls, logs, ditches, water holes, gates, fences—as if he'd had wings on his hooves. And, by the time he pulled up in front of the judges his breathing was heavy but far from labored. Kate saw the judges nod approvingly.

Kate immediately headed back to the barn. She

wanted to give Night Owl a handful of grain as an extra treat. She also wanted to have plenty of time to rest up for the stadium jumping after lunch. Dr. Andrews was just entering the barn when she came up.

"How's Elsinore . . . Ellie?" asked Kate.

"Not very well, I'm afraid," said Dr. Andrews gravely, and disappeared into the barn. Kate shivered. After the fire Ellie had been moved into a quieter stall in the back section of the barn, so that the commotion of the other horses wouldn't distress her. She must be really sick, thought Kate, rubbing Night Owl down, then making her way back outside to Pete, Jessie and Amory. Dara had gotten there ahead of her.

"That was a beautiful round," enthused Jessie. "Really tops."

"Thanks, Jess," said Kate.

"I mean, you have really improved up here," Jessie continued. "Both of you."

"Old Langwald worked our butts off, I tell you," Kate said. "But I guess it's done some good."

"I'll say," said Jessie. "I can't wait to bring Time Out up here next year."

"Have a hot dog," broke in Pete, smiling his admiration.

"Thanks," said Kate and jumped up on the hood of the car next to him. The sun was warm. There was a slight breeze that kept the edge off the heat and the air smelled of dust and horse sweat— familiar, delicious smells, Kate decided, digging into her hot dog. She was halfway through when Casey and Trevor came up. Kate had never seen Casey looking so happy. Trevor, too, for that matter.

"You must be Pete," said Trevor, coming over and shaking hands with Pete.

Pete looked at Kate in confusion as he held out his hand.

"This is my very dear friend, Trevor Williams," said Kate warmly.

"Kate's told me all about you," said Trevor.

Pete grinned and put his arm around Kate. "And I thought she'd forgotten all about me," he said.

"Anyone want another hot dog?" said Trevor. "The line was so long over at the stand, I figured I'd buy a bunch while I was there."

Eager hands grabbed up the food.

"Hey, save one for Caroline," said Kate. "She's headed this way."

"They just posted the cross-country scores," said Caroline, taking the offered hot dog.

"And?" said Dara and Kate in unison.

"I'm in fourth after the cross-country," said Caroline, breaking into a huge smile.

Everyone shouted and yipped and yahooed. Kate jumped off the car and gave her a hug. Caroline's smile just got bigger and bigger.

"And ..." She paused for dramatic effect. "Our current leader is Miss Kate Wiley, with a slight edge in points over Miss Dara Cooper."

Everyone seemed to be hugging each other at once.

"I guess the stadium jumping will be the deciding factor," Kate said.

"I guess so," said Dara.

"You don't want to go back into your blue funk by any chance," Kate teased Dara.

Dara laughed. "Sorry, but you did too good a job getting me out of it."

"You know," said Kate. "I don't really care about the blue ribbon so much. I just want to prove to Langwald I can do it."

"Kate Wiley, you're going to fight that poor man to the end," laughed Casey.

"He certainly never spared me," said Kate.

Kate knew she'd won the stadium jumping before she even finished the course. Night Owl sailed over the jumps with an unfailing stride. He hadn't even ticked a jump.

Dara and Casey had the next-best round, followed by Trevor. Pointwise, overall, Kate won the trials with Dara coming in second, and Casey third.

"So, are we going to the Olympics or what?" Dara cried out in high spirits as they headed back to the barn.

"Since we've survived Langwald's," responded Kate, "the Olympics will be a piece of cake."

Casey laughed. "I think we've just realized the big lesson old Fangwald has been trying to teach us."

"Yeah," said Kate. "All work and no play will make you crazy, but will get you to the Olympics!"

"I don't know if I can handle that. I'm wacko already," Dara said. "Do you think you can be that dedicated, Kate?"

"I'm going to try," Kate said eagerly. "Being here has given me a taste for the big time. I'm going for it."

"Me, too," said Casey. "What's making a spot

on the Olympic team after losing seventeen pounds!"

"What's the Olympics compared to good friends?" broke in Caroline.

"True, true," agreed the others. They started to dismount outside the barn. Just then Kate saw Dr. Andrews exit from a side door and head slowly toward his van.

"I'll be in in a second," said Kate, turning Night Owl toward the doctor.

"Dr. Andrews! Dr. Andrews," she called, riding up. His face looked drawn and haggard. "How's Ellie?"

Dr. Andrews dropped his head and didn't speak for a long moment. When he looked back up his eyes were wet with tears. "We had to put her down," he said, his voice breaking. "There was nothing more we could do."

Kate felt a sharp pain, almost as if she had lost her own horse. Speechless, she watched Dr. Andrews get into his van and drive away, her head filling with the image of the beautiful palomino on her bedroom wall—Elsinore of Bodiam.

Chapter 15

KATE took a deep breath and let it out slowly. Hamburgers! The night air smelled of charcoal and hamburgers. And she was starving. And happy. And tired. And sad. All that was left of her time at Langwald's was the cookout tonight and tomorrow's good-byes. Kate stopped brushing her hair for a minute and stared at her face in the mirror. Did she look any older? She sure felt it—and wiser and more independent—than she'd been at the beginning of camp. She'd survived her first separation from home. She'd made friends from strangers. She'd proven herself as a rider. She grinned at her reflection, threw on a pair of shorts and a T-shirt, then headed for the door. Before leaving her room, she paused once again in front of Ellie's picture.

"Thank you for being my friend this summer," she whispered reverently. "I hope your long life was a happy one."

A rousing cheer went up when she joined the others on the patio behind the main house. Everyone wanted to congratulate her for being the big winner of the day. Pete came up, put his arm around her and handed her a soda. Someone turned up the music. The lights strung around the patio twinkled like stars.

"Where's Langwald?" asked Casey, offering hamburgers from a plate stacked high. They were disappearing as fast as Caroline and Trevor could make them.

"I don't know," said Kate, not wanting to dim people's spirits by mentioning Ellie. "I guess he'll turn up later."

Much as she hated to admit it, Kate still wanted to face him. After all, he'd treated her like a failure all summer. And today she'd proven him wrong. What would he have to say about that? Kate grinned wickedly to herself.

"Kate! Kate?" someone called.

"Yes ... here," she replied.

"Langwald wants to see you ... in his office."

Kate swallowed hard and stared at Dara and Jessie. Suddenly, she wasn't so sure she could face him, win or no win.

"Well. Go on," urged Dara. "He probably wants to apologize for misjudging you."

"Hurry back and tell us all about it," said Jessie. "I want to know how many ways he can find to say *champion*."

Kate walked into the house, back through the rec room, down the long hall to the far wing of the house. It was quiet back here. The noise of the party hadn't filtered through. Kate paused to calm herself before knocking on the office door.

"Come in, Kate," said Langwald.

He was sitting behind his desk and motioned for Kate to have a seat on the sofa. Kate sat down, looking around the whole while. She'd never been in here before. No one had. The walls were lined with pictures of horses, many of them Ellie. Kate felt a wave of compassion for Langwald. His favorite horse had been put to sleep that very day. He must be very sad inside.

"Kate, I wanted to congratulate you on your performance today," he began in his deep, resonant voice.

"Thank you, Mr. Langwald," said Kate, thrilled that he would actually recognize her accomplishments.

"Pietro Yon told me you were an extraordinary rider," he continued. "But I'd like to add to that. You're one of the best who's ever come through this school, and some of my students are currently on the U.S. team."

Kate's ears burned. She couldn't believe it. She'd won. She'd finally made him see her for what she was, but she was still confused.

"Why were you always criticizing me then?" she asked.

"Oh Kate," he said in exasperation. "I wasn't criticizing *you*. You kept wanting to hear it that way, because you didn't want to hear that it was Night Owl who wasn't making it." He shifted in his seat, then added in a gentler tone, "I'm afraid I also have to agree with Pietro that you're not going to get much further without another horse."

"Wh ... what!" stammered Kate, rising halfway from the sofa in shock. "Night Owl did beautifully today! How can you say that!"

"Yes, I agree," Langwald said. "He did a magnificent job. But he's too inconsistent. I've been watching him. He does great one day then wants to play the next. You can't afford to gamble on his mood at the level at which you're now riding. You need the best horse possible."

"No!" cried Kate, her insides churning with emotion. Langwald was suggesting she get rid of Night Owl? And Mr. Yon, her Pietro, was in cahoots with him! Kate felt betrayed. "No!" she cried in desperation. "I know he's a little moody, but he's getting better. Didn't you notice over this month?"

Langwald shook his head. "No. I noticed you getting better and better but being held back by your horse."

"I'll work him extra hard," pleaded Kate. "He's super smart. I'll have him pulled around in no time."

"He's seven years old, Kate," said Mr. Langwald gently. "He's not going to change. My advice is to sell him to someone starting in the novice division and get yourself a horse like Arpeggio."

"No, Mr. Langwald," said Kate, anger now overcoming her disbelief. She stood up and started for the door. "Night Owl is *my* horse. We're going to the Olympics together."

Kate stalked out of the room and started down the long hallway, tears blurring her way. Then suddenly, in her head, she heard Dr. Andrews: "He loves that horse. Everyone told him she wasn't Olympic material. . . . He gave up fame for her."

Kate turned around and went back to Langwald's office. She pushed open the door without knocking. He was still at his desk, but his head was buried in his hands. When he looked up, tears stood out in his eyes.

"I ... I'm terribly sorry about Ellie, Mr. Langwald," Kate said.

Langwald stared at her for what seemed like the longest time. Kate stared back at his sad face.

"Thank you, Kate," he said finally, his voice gravelly with emotion. "You of all people must understand exactly what I'm feeling."

Pete found her in Night Owl's stall half an hour later. She had her head resting against him and her arms around his neck.

"Kate?" said Pete gently. "Kate, what's wrong?"

Kate looked at him with large, red-rimmed eyes and sighed deeply.

Pete hesitated at the door of the stall. "I've been looking everywhere for you. I ... I was worried." He took an uncertain step toward her. "Are you okay?"

Kate continued to stare at his face wreathed in concern. Five second ago she'd felt totally alone in the world. Everyone—her mother, Pietro, Langwald, even Dara and Jessie—had failed her. They all wanted her to sell Night Owl. But here was Pete, and he cared. She held out her hand to him.

"Oh Pete," she said, but couldn't continue. The words wouldn't form in her mouth.

"What is it, Kate?" he coaxed, putting an arm around her. "Please tell me. I can't stand to see you looking so sad."

Suddenly Kate burst into tears. She clung to Pete. "They ... all of them ... want me to get rid of Night Owl."

"Whoa," he said. "What do you mean, *get rid* of him?"

"They ... Langwald ... Mr. Langwald," said Kate through her sobs, "told me I had to have another horse if I'm ever going to get any further in my riding. He told me to sell Night Owl!" Kate dissolved into sobs. Pete held her closer.

"Oh, Kate!" he said. "That's terrible. It's just terrible."

"I can't give up Night Owl, Pete," sobbed Kate. "I just can't. He's my best friend in all the world." She looked up at Pete. "Except you." She continued to stare at him. "I mean that, Pete."

Pete chuckled softly and kissed her head. "You know, I don't mind being rated next to Night Owl. I consider that pretty high up in the world."

Kate smiled through her tears and put her arms around Pete's neck. He brushed the loose hairs away from her face.

"Kate? You know I don't know a whole lot about horses and all this stuff. But I want you to know I'm here for you. I'll help you any way I can. Okay?"

Kate had never been pulled from such sadness to such happiness in all her life. Warmth and life began to seep back into her heart.

"I'm going to need you, Pete," she said quietly. "A whole lot."

"That's fine with me," he said gently, hugging her tightly. "I'll be right here."

Night Owl nickered softly beside them.

GLOSSARY

BIT. A metal or rubber bar that is fit into the horse's mouth to help control the horse's direction and speed; part of the bridle.

BLAZE. A striking white marking of medium width that runs down the middle of a horse's face.

BREECHES. Riding pants, usually of a tight stretch material, that fit closely over the calves and are worn inside riding boots.

BROODMARE. Female horse used specifically for breeding.

BRIDLE. Headgear consisting of head and throat straps, bit, and reins. Used for controlling a horse.

CANTER. A rolling three-beat gait, faster than a trot.

CAVALLETTI. A series of long poles of adjustable height, supported by crossbars; used in teaching both horses and riders to jump.

CONFORMATION. A horse's proportionate shape or contour.

CRIB. A type of bin used to hold food for stable animals; "cribbing" is also a bad habit of horses who bite the edges of doors, feed bins, etc. while sucking in air.

CROSS-COUNTRY. A timed event that takes place on open land. These courses include riding across fields, through woods, and along trails, and require jumping over natural and man-made barriers such as ditches, logs, and hedges.

CROSS-TIES. A pair of leads, one attached to the right side of the halter and one to the left, used for holding the horse in place while grooming.

CURRY. To rub and clean a horse with a *curry comb,* which is a round rubber comb that loosens mud, dried sweat, and hair.

DIAGONAL. In riding, refers to the rider's position at the posting trot as the horse moves diagonal pairs of legs. On a circle, the rider would be rising in the saddle as the horse's outside shoulder moves forward (and the inside shoulder moves back). This keeps the rider from interfering with the horse's balance and freedom of movement.

DRESSAGE. Training a horse to perform with increased balance, suppleness, and obedience, and to perfect its paces. A dressage test involves a traditional system of complex maneuvers performed in an arena in front of one or more judges. The test is scored on each movement and on the overall impression that horse and rider make.

EVENT. Also known as a *Horse Trial.* A competitive series of exercises which test a horse's strength, obedience, and intelligence. Also used as a verb: "Now she has a horse of her own to ride and *event.*"

EVENTING. Also known as *combined training* and *three-day eventing*. A series of tests combining dressage, jumping, and cross-country competitions.

FARRIER. A person who shoes horses; a blacksmith.

FETLOCK. The horse's ankle; a projection bearing a tuft of hair on the back of a horse's leg, above the hoof and the pastern.

FILLY. A female horse less than four years of age.

FLANK. On a horse, the fleshy part of the side between the ribs and the hip.

FOAL. A horse under one year of age. Foals are usually weaned at six months and are then called weanlings. Also, to give birth to a horse.

FOALING BOX. A structure used as a maternity ward for expectant mares, usually designed with a gap in the wall so that labor and birth may be observed secretly.

GAITS. General term for all the foot movements of a horse: walk, trot, canter, or gallop.

GALLOP. The horse's fastest gait, although there are gradations; an open gallop is faster than a hard gallop.

GELDING. A male horse that has been castrated for the purpose of improving the animal's temper and health.

GIRTH. A sturdy strap and buckle for securing the saddle.

GROOM. To clean and care for an animal. Also the person who performs these tasks.

HALT. In dressage, bringing the horse to an absolute stop with all four feet square and straight.

HALF-HALT. A subtle signal that encourages the horse to gather himself, improving his balance and preparing him for a change of pace or direction.

HALTER. A loose-fitting headgear with a noseband and head and throat straps to which a lead line may be attached.

HANDS. A unit used to measure a horse's height, each hand equaling 4 inches. A horse is measured from the ground to his withers. Ponies stand up to 14 hands 2 inches (14½ hands high); larger horses are everything above. A 15-hand horse stands 5 feet high at his withers.

HAYRACK. A rack for holding hay for feeding horses.

HOOF-PICK. A piece of grooming equipment used to gently clean dirt and stones from between hoof and horseshoe.

IMPULSION. The horse shows willingness to move freely, particularly through the powerful driving action of its hindquarters.

IN AND OUT. Two fences positioned close to each other and related in distance, so that the horse must jump "in" over the first fence and "out" over second.

JODHPURS. Riding pants cut full through the hips and fitted closely from knee to ankle.

JUMPING. In eventing, also known as *stadium jumping*. Horse and rider must take and clear ten to twelve fences in a ring. Penalty points are added for refusals, falls, and knockdowns.

LATERAL MOVEMENT. When a horse moves sideways and forward at the same time.

LEAD. The piece of rope or leather used to lead a horse.

LIPPIZANER. A compact, handsome horse, usually gray, originally bred at the Lippiza Stud near Trieste; famous for their use in dressage exhibitions at the Spanish Riding School in Vienna.

MUCKING OUT. To clear manure and soiled bedding from a horse stall.

OXER. A jump or obstacle that requires the horse to jump width as well as height.

PADDOCK. An enclosed outdoor area where horses are turned out and exercised.

PACE. The speed at which a horse travels, or, in harness racing, a two-beat gait in which the legs on the same side of the horse move in unison.

PALOMINO. Technically a color rather than a breed; a type of horse developed mainly in the southwestern United States. These animals have golden coats and flaxen or white manes and tails.

POST. Rising up and down out of the saddle in rhythm with the horse's trot.

SADDLE FLAPS. Side pieces on an English saddle. They hide the straps needed to keep the saddle in place.

SERPENTINE. In dressage, a series of equal curves from one side of the ring's center line to the other. The horse changes the direction of his turn each time he passes over the center line.

SHOULDER. A lateral movement in which the horse moves sideways and forward at the same time, bending his body around the rider's leg.

STANDARD. An upright post used to support the rail of a hurdle.

STIRRUP LEATHER. The strap used to suspend a stirrup from a saddle.

TACK. The gear used to outfit a horse for riding, such as saddle, halter, and bridle.

TROT. A two-beat gait faster than a walk, in which the horse's legs move in diagonal pairs (left forward, right rear).

WITHERS. The ridge between a horse's shoulder bones. The highest point above the shoulders where the neck joins the back.

Turn over for a sneak preview of GOLDEN GIRL,
the fourth book in Bantam's BLUE RIBBON series.

Dara posted as the big grey moved under her. The summer morning air breezed by her face, and she caught the smell of dry grass mixed with the dust of the ring. She lost herself briefly in the rhythm of riding, and the thought of how wonderful a horse was.

"You're losing him, Dara, watch his shoulders on the corners." Anne's voice startled Dara and she brought her attention back to Arpeggio. "Keep him coming forward, that's it, but don't let him rush the corners."

Dara hadn't realized that's what he was doing. She stopped posting and did a sitting trot, so she would have more contact with the saddle and be more aware of what Arpeggio was doing. A fine mist of perspiration formed on her forehead. Even with the ring still shaded it was hot. If the fates were fair, the air conditioning in Doug's car would have broken down and he and Gloria would be sweating too. She hoped all of Gloria's mascara was running down her cheeks. All the unhappiness she had felt at the news of Gloria and Doug dating each other came back to her with a rush.

"Dara, you're letting him take control. Make him wait for you. Your left hand is dropping again, move your thumb and bend your elbow. Keep him coming forward. There, that's better. Can you feel the difference?"

Dara nodded, but the truth was she couldn't, she couldn't feel much of anything except a rush of anger every time she thought of Doug.

What was Anne Wiley trying to tell her? She forced herself to pay attention to what she was doing, and she succeeded for almost a full minute before Doug and Gloria took over again. She had a picture of them in the roller coaster, Gloria hanging on to Doug for all she was worth.

"If you're going to loosen the rein, you have to sit back and control him with your legs and seat," Anne called.

"I know," Dara shot back sharply. "I know. Give me a chance."

"Don't go forward with him when he speeds up," Anne said.

"I know that too," Dara said angrily. "That's practically the first thing I learned." She could feel Anne's eyes on her but she refused to meet them.

"But you're not controlling him, Dara. I wouldn't be doing my job if I didn't point it out."

Grimly Dara adjusted her position again, and this time Arpeggio came to a faltering halt and then when she applied her leg to him, took off at a trot instead of the canter they had been doing. "What's the matter with him?" she asked in exasperation.

"Nothing," Anne said. "Let him walk a minute and you try and calm down. This heat has probably gotten to you."

"He's not listening to me," Dara said as she walked Arpeggio around the ring on a loose rein.

"You're not telling him much," Anne said.

"What's that mean?"

"Well, your form's a little sloppy," Anne said trying to be kind. "You're not as straight and alert as you usually are. I didn't think you looked well when you came into the ring. I don't know, you're kind of slouching, the line from the bit to your elbow is wrong and you're leaning forward too much. Kate used to do that, but ..."

Dara stared at Anne and felt a rush of anger that took in the whole world. "I am paying attention," she interrupted. "I'm riding him the way I've always ridden him. Maybe seeing Kate on Spy has made every other horse and rider in the world look terrible to you."

"Dara," Anne said surprised.

"I rode for an entire month at Langwald's and he didn't complain about the way I rode or the way Arpeggio went."

"Not at all?" Anne said.

"Not at all," Dara told her.

"Then you didn't get your money's worth," Anne said.

The tears that had pricked Dara's eyes earlier in the barn, were back. She held her lids rigidly open, so they wouldn't spill down her cheeks and embarrass her in front of Anne. "Mrs. Wiley," she said with as much control as she could muster, "You were right, I'm not feeling well. I'd just as soon cancel this lesson," and before Anne could say a word, Dara left the ring.